things Change

"Camilla, what's gotten into you?" Mom asked. "We're changing some of our traditions to make it easier on your grandfather. He's having a hard enough time without being reminded every minute during the Christmas season of something your grandmother did with us. I'm surprised at your quick tongue, and I'm disappointed."

"I don't care. I don't understand this at all. It just isn't fair to change all the best traditions. Grandpa's going to hate it and be even more sad because we're forgetting every good thing we did with Grandma. We're forgetting Grandma."

Callie ran out of the kitchen and up the steps to her bedroom.

"Hey, shrimp, what's the matter with you?" Clint greeted her at the top of the stairs.

"Nothing. Just be prepared for the worst Christmas ever," she cried, slamming her door behind her.

The Worst Christmas Ever

Connie Remlinger-Trounstine

The Worst Christmas Ever

Connie Remlinger-Trounstine

Rainbow Bridge®

Troll Associates

*To my family and my extended family
and all their traditions*

chapter 1

Callie Thomas pulled her green plaid scarf tighter around her neck as she hurried through the cold rain.

"Hey, Mr. Gordon, you better watch out. You'll get sopping wet and catch a cold," she shouted to the school janitor. He was standing on a ladder, stringing colored lights on the tall evergreen tree in front of the school.

"Just a couple more minutes and I'll be finished, Callie," he called back. "All this work will be worth it when you see this tree with all the lights on. Wish the rain would turn to snow."

"I don't," Callie mumbled. "I wish it were January and Christmas was over, so I didn't have to listen to everyone say what a great time of the year it is."

Callie hurried into the building. She hung her wet coat in her locker and sat down at her desk just as the bell rang.

Mrs. Peterson rapped her hand on the podium and got right down to business.

"Class, it's time for today's oral reports on Christmas traditions. Yesterday, we went to Sanibel Island off the coast of Florida where Mark spends Christmas with his grandparents. His family traditionally goes snorkeling on Christmas Day. He was kind enough to bring each of us a shell he'd picked up along the beach."

Mrs. Peterson looked over at Mark and smiled. "Today, we are going skiing at Alta, Utah, outside Salt Lake City, with Bethany Clark's family. The temperature in Alta on a typical Christmas Day is five degrees compared to eighty degrees in Florida."

Everyone sat quietly as Bethany made her way to the front of the room with her skis and boots. Callie leaned into the aisle, not wanting to miss anything.

Bethany was the first person Callie had talked to on her first day at Dexter School. Callie had been standing by her locker, trying to figure out which way to go to find Room 107-A. Her mother had dropped her off early so that she would have time to get oriented. But she'd spent so much time looking for her locker that now she was going to be late for class. The hall clock showed she had two minutes before the bell rang.

"You look lost," a voice from behind her had said.

"I am," she had said, turning. "Can you point me in the direction of Room 107-A?"

"That's where I'm going. Follow me."

"Thanks."

"My name is Bethany Clark. You're new, I can tell. Did you just move to the city?"

Before Callie could answer, a book that she was trying to balance in one arm as she adjusted her purse strap with her other hand slipped to the floor. She stooped to pick it up and somehow lost her balance. Suddenly she found herself on the floor looking up.

"Are you okay? Are you hurt?" Bethany asked, gathering the books that had gone flying when Callie hit the floor.

"Nothing hurt but my pride, as my grandpa would say," Callie said with an embarrassed smile. She took her books from Bethany.

"What's this?" Bethany said, holding up a brown paper bag as if it was a foreign object.

"My lunch."

"Guess no one told you. We all eat together in the cafeteria. No one brings their lunch."

Callie followed Bethany down the hallway to the classroom.

"I think you need help," Bethany said. "Wait for me after class and I'll show you the way to math."

Bethany was different from all the girls Callie

knew at the county school. She wore coordinated skirts and sweaters and sometimes her shoes even matched her outfit. And she never called anyone "creep" like Nora Miller did all the time. Nora was Callie's best friend at the county school.

Bethany was very mature for her age. Callie wanted to be her friend more than anything else in the world.

In fact, getting to know girls like Bethany was why Callie had begged her parents to send her to Dexter, a private school in the city. The kids there all seemed so glamorous and sophisticated. Callie hoped some of their confidence would rub off on her.

"Last year my father gave my brother and me brand-new ski boots," Bethany explained, holding up the bright red boot in front of the class. "A pump on the front is attached to a small inner tube inside. You inflate the tube to get a snug fit around your ankle so you don't get hurt if you fall."

Callie looked around the room. Everyone's eyes were glued on Bethany and the boots. Callie could tell they were impressed. Bethany was the most popular girl in sixth grade.

"Thank you, Bethany, for sharing your Christmas holiday with us and giving us some new and interesting information on skiing," Mrs. Peterson said when Bethany had finished. "We have a few more minutes before the bell rings. I'm sure Bethany will be happy to answer any of your questions."

Almost everyone in the class skied. In fact, skiing was so popular at Dexter that they even offered a weekend trip to the Adirondack Mountains in New York state.

"Are you going on the ski trip after Christmas?" Peter Hall asked Callie as they stood next to each other, watching Ambrose Chandler try to put his size nine foot into the size six boot.

Peter Hall was the cutest boy in the class. Callie thought he was even cuter than her brother Johnny. Peter had thick hair and he was very tall. He always wore crewneck sweaters and loafers. Everyone at Dexter wore loafers. Callie knew she was getting a pair for Christmas.

Callie could feel her face getting hot. She always blushed the same color as her auburn hair when she was nervous or embarrassed or when she stretched the truth a little bit.

"I haven't decided yet."

That wasn't true. There was no way her parents could afford $400 to send her on a weekend trip to New York. She was already lining up babysitting jobs to earn enough money to go on the class trip to Washington, D.C., next year.

"My family is so busy right now with the holidays that I haven't asked about the skiing trip," she said.

At least that was true. She didn't add that the one

and only thing her family did at this time of the year was sell Christmas trees.

Grandpa John had started the family business in West Virginia more than fifty years ago. Callie's father, Joe, carried on the tradition in Cincinnati, Ohio.

The Christmas season for her family began a week before Thanksgiving Day. That's when trucks filled with trees cut in North Carolina pulled into the long lane that led back to their farmhouse. Everybody in the family—Grandma and Grandpa, Callie's mother and father and brothers, and Grandpa's brother, who everyone called Uncle Tony, helped unload the trucks filled with long-needled white pine, Scotch pine, and short-needled balsam and Fraser firs.

No one in the family escaped the work at Christmastime. Even three-year-old Jason was expected to cooperate. Everyone was too busy, too tired, and too crabby to play with him the way they did the rest of the year.

Callie used to love the Christmas season. Now she dreaded it. Sixth grade meant a lot more homework. She had an important part in the school's Christmas program. And she was working on a science project, too!

There was another reason why Christmas promised to be terrible for her family. It would be their first one without Grandma Mary, who had died in July. Callie couldn't imagine Christmas without Grandma. For as long as she could remember, Grandma was always there, baking cookies, decorating the tree, stuffing the turkey.

Callie gathered up her books from the desk and walked toward the door. What could she ever talk about for her speech? The only thing her family did at Christmastime was work.

I can just see getting up there and talking about riding with Grandpa in his antique pickup truck to the lot at the corner of Hatch and Eighth Streets, she thought. The idea was so silly she had to smile. But she was beginning to wonder if going to private school might not have been the biggest mistake of her life.

"Camilla, wait for me," Bethany yelled from down the hall.

Callie's real name was Camilla, but everyone in her family—except her brother Johnny—called her Callie. Sometimes Mom and Dad would say "Camilla" when they were upset with her, and Grandpa would say "Now, Camilla" when he was making a point about something. But none of the kids at Dexter knew her nickname.

"Great speech," Callie said, stopping to wait for Bethany. "Altoon sounds like a really nice place to go skiing."

"Alta, not Altoon, silly," Bethany corrected.

Bethany pointed out other people's errors a lot. Callie didn't let it bother her. Bethany was just a very blunt person, the way Grandpa was sometimes.

"Our family almost went skiing in Vermont last year," Callie said. "But we had to change our plans at the last minute."

That was a lie. Her cousins Annie and Bridget did almost go skiing. Callie felt as bad as they did when the trip was canceled. That kind of empathy had to count for something.

"Bethany. Camilla. Wait for us," Ann Layman called.

"I love your ski boots, Bethany," Monica Lance said as she and Ann fell into step beside them.

"Me, too," Ann said. "I'm going to ask Mom and Dad for a pair for Christmas so I'll have them for the ski trip."

"I didn't know you were going on the trip, Ann," Monica said. "Are you, Bethany? Are you, Camilla?"

"I think I am," Bethany said.

The three girls looked at Camilla. "Well, umm, I'm not sure yet," she lied.

❖ ❖ ❖

Later in the day, Callie, hunched down in her coat, waited outside the school for her mother to pick her up. Bethany came out and walked toward her.

"I was wondering if you could come over to my house on the nineteenth, the Saturday before Christmas, and stay overnight?" Bethany asked unexpectedly. "My parents always allow me to invite one friend over that weekend. We go skating at the Ice Bowl, then back to my house."

Callie couldn't believe it. Just last week she'd dreamed she was sleeping in Bethany's white canopy bed. She had never been in Bethany's bedroom, but she was sure Bethany had a bed with a canopy. She lived in a beautiful old Tudor house set back off a tree-lined street just three blocks from school.

"I don't know," Callie said as nonchalantly as she could. Her heart was pounding in her chest. "I'll have to ask Mom."

Then she crossed her fingers to cover up the lie. "I'm almost one hundred percent sure she'll let me."

She could feel the blood rushing to her face.

"Good. I'll tell my mother you can come."

Callie watched Bethany walk up the street until she was out of sight. The Saturday before Christmas was the busiest day of the year for selling trees. If they didn't make enough money selling trees, she probably wouldn't be able to return to Dexter next year. Private schools cost a lot of money. Her parents had put off remodeling the kitchen to send her this year.

Callie knew she would have to work that Saturday. But she couldn't say no to Bethany. She had waited too long for an invitation. She would do anything to be best friends with Bethany.

"I'll just have to think of something," she said aloud.

chapter 2

Callie sat on the school steps, her chin in her hands, staring into space. Usually she read her English or history assignments while she waited for her mother to pick her up.

Today she couldn't concentrate.

The chirping of a pair of cardinals caught her attention. She watched them play tag, flitting from one buckeye tree to another. But she quickly lost interest.

"I have to find some way to go to Bethany's house," she said to herself as her mother pulled into the school parking lot.

"You're late," Callie snapped. She climbed into the front seat, pulling the door shut.

"Honey, you knew I would be. I told you this morning I wanted to stop downtown to pick up a wooden train set for Jason."

Mom was right. She had said she would be late.

But with everything else on her mind, Callie had forgotten. She opened her mouth to say she was sorry but she couldn't make the words come out. Instead, she listened to Mom talk about the train.

Callie leaned back against the seat and turned her head toward her mother. She thought, as she had so many times before, that her mother was beautiful.

Callie had inherited her red hair and fair skin. But the similarity ended there. Her mother's hair was curly and she had soft brown eyes. Callie's hair was straight as sticks, and she had her father's and grandfather's snapping blue eyes.

Callie's mother was petite. Come to think of it, Bethany was petite, too. So were all the popular girls at school.

Callie was tall and skinny. Her mother often told her that she was lucky because she could wear clothes like a model. Callie didn't care. She had already made up her mind to be a baby doctor, or maybe a writer or a photographer. And all that mattered now was that she was the tallest person in her class, except for Peter Hall.

As Mom talked, Callie turned to look out the window. She watched the towboat guide a long line of barges through the dark, choppy waters of the Ohio River. She loved the excitement of the city, but she never tired of watching the river that snaked along the country road to her home.

Mom slowed the van as she put on her blinker to turn onto Turtle Creek Road.

"Right on schedule, just two weeks before Christmas, your father and grandfather are arguing," Mom said.

"Wait, let me tell you why," Callie said. "Grandpa says we should order more trees from North Carolina."

Mom nodded.

The argument was the same every year. Grandpa always insisted they buy more trees. Her dad, who was more conservative, didn't want to buy more than he was sure they could sell. Either way was a gamble.

"Grandpa is usually right," Callie said, smiling as she pictured his twinkling eyes and snow-white hair.

Grandpa John and Grandma Mary were both born in Italy. They came to America with their families when they were teenagers. They met one day when Grandma went into Grandpa's market to buy fresh fish.

"She was the prettiest girl I had ever seen," he would tell his grandchildren. "I didn't have the kind of fish she wanted, but I drove my father's car to the next town to get it for her. It gave me a good excuse to go to her house and ask her for a date."

Along with selling seafood and groceries in the market, Grandpa sold Christmas trees to add to the family income. He tried to talk his three sons into growing trees at their homes. Callie's dad was the only son who did.

Callie remembered the weekend her grandparents came to Ohio to plant the first seedlings.

"These seeds will grow into strong, sturdy fir and pine trees just about the time you're ready to go to high school," Grandma had told Callie.

The trees were now about two feet taller than Jason.

Not long after they had planted the seedlings, Grandpa suffered a heart attack and had to sell his market. A year later, Grandma telephoned Callie's father to ask if he would consider selling trees in Ohio.

After this conversation with Grandma, Dad had called a family meeting. Everyone gathered around the old wooden table in the kitchen where they made all major family decisions.

"Grandma says all Grandpa does is sit around the house and mope. He needs to be doing something with his time, but he's not strong enough to handle the lots in West Virginia alone any more. If we leased lots here, we could all help him. Grandpa's brother Tony could come from his home in Maine to help."

Callie thought it was a great idea. It meant Grandma and Grandpa and Uncle Tony would live with them for at least a month. Her brothers, Johnny and Clint, who were both older than Callie, thought it would be a great adventure. Jason hadn't even been born yet.

Mom was more cautious. "It's a lot of work and you'll all have to pitch in and help, even when it isn't fun," she cautioned them.

Despite the warning, the family voted unanimously to go into the tree business.

Callie was too young to help on the lots when they first started. Instead, she stayed home to help Grandma.

Grandma taught Callie how to cook and knit. One year she taught her how to sing "Silent Night" in Italian as a special Christmas gift for Grandpa. She sang it for him on Christmas Eve after they had finished decorating the tree. It was the only time Callie had ever seen her grandpa cry.

What would this Christmas be like without Grandma?

As Callie and her mother neared their house, Callie leaned into the backseat to get her books.

"Mom, do you think Dad will need me at the lots all the time this year?"

"What a silly question, Callie. You know how much your father and grandfather depend on you."

"Oh, I know. I was just asking."

Callie took a bag of groceries from the back of the van and carried it to the kitchen table. She took off her coat and hung it on a hook in the mud room. As she started toward the living room, a bright red-and-green striped envelope lying on the counter caught her eye. It had her name on it. The bold, round letters looked familiar.

"Hey, creep, who'd you get the card from?" her brother Clint asked as he poured himself a glass of milk.

"None of your business, dork," she said, walking out of the room and letting the door swing back to hit him in the face.

"What's the matter? Is it a card from a boy?" he asked, pushing the door open and following her into the living room.

Callie ran up the steps to her bedroom and slammed the door behind her. "Why is my business everybody else's business in this family?" she said aloud.

She plopped her books down on her red-and-yellow polka-dot bedspread and took a closer look at the envelope. Then she opened it carefully.

Slowly she pulled out a card that had a wide red border. Printed in green letters was:

Please come to a party
on December 20 at the home
of Ann Layman
6 p.m. to 10 p.m.
Dress casual.

Callie blinked and read the card again. Was it for real? Ann Layman was the most popular girl in school next to Bethany!

Callie touched the card to make sure she wasn't dreaming. "Ann Layman invited me to a party," she said aloud. "Me!"

"Who's your card from, double creep?" Clint asked again as he walked into her room.

"None of your beeswax," she snarled.

"Ooh, looks like an invitation," he said, twisting his head to read the card she was holding in her hand. "Mom will never let you go," he concluded.

"What do you mean? Of course she will."

"Never. Look at the date. It's December twentieth. Nobody, but nobody, in this family does anything but sell trees the weekend before Christmas."

Callie hadn't thought about the date. Sure enough, the card said December 20.

"Get out of my room," Callie shouted, pushing Clint toward the door. "Get out of my life."

Callie flung herself face down on the bed and

began to cry. All semester long she had been trying to be friends with Bethany and Ann and Monica. She knew she had started off on the wrong foot—literally—when she went crashing to the floor in the hallway on the first day of classes. At first they treated her like a person from outer space who was invading their territory.

Although no one ever told her, she knew Ann had a Halloween party but didn't invite her. No one said anything to her face, but Callie couldn't help overhearing everyone talk about it.

But since November things were getting better. She and Monica were picked to direct one of the vignettes that their class was presenting at the Christmas program. Most of the classes planned to sing or dance. But Mrs. Peterson had challenged her sixth graders to come up with something different. After a lot of debate, they decided to act out some holiday customs.

Peter and Dennis were in charge of a vignette about holiday food and drink. Bethany and Ann chose Hanukkah as their topic.

Callie and Monica decided to write about mistletoe. They had stayed after school three times looking up information in the library and then writing the script.

The fun part had been picking the three classmates who would be featured in the vignette.

They held auditions and decided Patty Cottington would represent mistletoe because she studied ballet and they needed someone who could climb up and down a ladder gracefully.

They picked Melissa Williams for the girl's part because she was very pretty, with beautiful long, blond hair. But they couldn't agree on who should play the male role.

"I think we should ask Ambrose Chandler," Callie had said.

Ambrose was the only boy in the sixth grade who had a burr haircut. It accentuated his big ears. His dreamy blue eyes were always staring into space as though he was in another world, and he usually wore a silly smirk on his face. He couldn't keep his shirt tucked into his pants and he managed to trip over his own feet or somebody else's at least once a day.

"Ambrose! He's a nerd," Monica had said.

"Exactly!"

They had doubled up with laughter, just thinking about Ambrose kissing Melissa.

"Camilla, you're so clever. And he can't say no if we ask him," Monica had said, giving Callie a high five.

Now she was invited to Ann's party and to stay overnight at Bethany's house—on the worst possible weekend. Clint was right. Selling Christmas trees was the only thing that her family thought about at this time of the year.

But Callie couldn't say no to the most popular girls in school. If she did, she would never be invited to anything again.

chapter 3

Callie closed her eyes and drifted off to sleep. Before long she saw herself sitting in a blue velvet high-backed chair in the dining room of Bethany's Tudor home. Everybody was there: Ann, Monica, Peter, even Ambrose. Bethany was at the head of the long oak table.

A large crystal chandelier twinkled like hundreds of multicolored diamonds. A tall white pine tree decorated with gold and red balls glowed in a corner of the living room.

Everyone was dressed up. Callie had on her new purple sweater and skirt. Peter, who was sitting across from her, was wearing a blue crewneck sweater and brown corduroy pants. She peeked under the table to see if he had on loafers. He did.

Then she glanced at her own feet and couldn't believe her eyes. She had on brown rubber boots that were caked with mud.

Bethany tapped her long-stemmed crystal water glass.

"I want to thank you all for coming. As a special treat tonight, my father had fresh lobsters flown in from Maine. It's my favorite meal. I know you all will like it, too."

Callie looked around. All her friends were nodding their heads and wearing broad smiles.

A man wearing a black tuxedo and top hat stepped forward. He lifted his trumpet and blew the charge heard at football games.

Men wearing white jackets and black pants marched out of the kitchen. Each carried a huge silver tray with a bright red lobster sitting in a bed of lettuce. The lobsters' beady brown eyes stared into space.

"Those are the most disgusting-looking animals I've ever seen in my whole life," Callie said. "I think I'm going to throw up."

No one paid any attention to her.

Peter was using a silver nutcracker to break open his lobster's claws.

Bethany had a piece of red-and-white lobster meat on a tiny fork. She daintily dipped it into a small bowl filled with melted butter.

Ann's grin stretched from one side of her face to the other. Callie got that same look on her face when Mom put a plate of homemade brownies on the table.

Callie sat very still and looked down at the lobster in front of her. It moved. She jumped up and her chair went flying. She put one foot up on the table, knocking over water glasses. She stuck her other foot in the punch bowl.

"Get your muddy boots off my mother's Irish linen tablecloth," Bethany screamed. "You're embarrassing me. I'm sorry I invited you. Go back to the county school where you belong!"

Callie tried to say she was sorry but she couldn't open her mouth. The lobster was biting her boot.

"Callie, Callie, wake up." Her mother's voice broke into her dream. Callie opened her eyes. She was in her own bedroom.

"Callie, do you hear me? It's time to eat."

"I'll be right there, Mom."

Callie hurried to the bathroom to splash cold water on her face. "What a nightmare!" she mumbled.

Dad, Grandpa, and Uncle Tony were discussing trees when Callie walked into the kitchen. She went to the refrigerator to get the milk.

"I think we should wait a day or two before we order more trees," Dad said.

"Joe, I remember ten years ago when we had a winter just like this one. It was exceptionally mild the first of December. Then it turned bitter cold and everyone was in the Christmas spirit. Remember that, Tony?"

Grandpa and his youngest brother had sold Christmas trees for more years than her father had lived. "Couldn't forget it. We sold out of trees. It was our best year," Uncle Tony said.

"Dad, if I go ahead with the order and buy the trees, it will make the difference between a profit and a loss. I've got Johnny in college and Callie in private school. I just don't know if I have the right to risk it."

"Don't forget me," Clint piped up. "You'll have to pay money for me to go to the Olympics in track."

Callie looked at Clint. He's really dreaming if he thinks he's good enough to run in the Olympics, she thought. Oh, well, let him dream. I've got more important things to worry about. I've got to wait for the perfect moment to ask to go to Bethany's house.

After the nightmare, she had decided not to go to Ann's party. They might serve lobster and then where would I be, Callie thought, turning up her nose in disgust. Just thinking about the lobster made Callie gag. She had trouble swallowing her mother's meatloaf.

"Don't you feel well, Callie? You've hardly touched a thing," Mom said.

"I'm okay, Mom. Just not very hungry."

Mom got up from the table. "Let's see. Clint, this is Friday so it's your day to clear the table and help with the dishes."

Clint slouched in his chair. "Aw, Mom. I just did 'em last night for Callie."

"That was because Callie bathed Jason and put him to bed while your father and I went to a meeting at the school."

Callie waited just long enough to make Clint suffer. Then she stood up and carried her plate to the sink.

"Oh, Mom, let the complainer go. I'll help."

Both Mom and Clint looked at Callie in amazement. Callie made no secret of the fact that she hated putting dishes into the dishwasher more than anything in the whole world.

"You know you don't have to. It's Clint's night," her mother said.

"That's okay. I want to help." She needed time alone with her mother.

Callie took the glasses from the table and put them in the top rack of the dishwasher.

"Mom, could you buy some extra butter when you go to the grocery store this weekend? I'm going to make the butter cookies that Grandma and I used to make. I still have all her cookie cutters in my dresser drawer."

"I don't know if we'll be making those cookies this year."

Callie froze. "What do you mean?"

"Your father and I have been talking. This will be our first Christmas without Grandma. We thought it might be easier if we didn't bring up all the memories at Christmastime."

Callie shook her head in disbelief. She might complain a lot about selling trees, but there were certain Christmas traditions that she didn't want to change in any way.

Callie never went to the lots on Christmas Eve. Instead she stayed home with Grandma Mary to help her get ready for the evening. As soon as everyone had left in the morning, they began baking butter cookies. Year after year, Callie watched Grandma's hands, twisted with arthritis, move the rolling pin to the center of the dough and back again, round and round in a circle.

"The secret to making good cookies is in the rolling," Grandma would say in her soft, melodious voice. "The dough can't be too thick or too thin."

Just last Christmas, Grandma handed Callie the rolling pin. "It's time for you to learn."

Grandma made it look a lot easier than it was. You had to have the right amount of flour on the board and the rolling pin or the dough would stick. If the dough was too thick, the cookies looked like a glob of Play-Doh and weren't baked in the middle. Other cookies were as thin as a piece of paper and burned.

Callie was persistent, and Grandma had patience. The last batch she rolled out was cut into angel shapes. They were perfect.

After the last cookie was iced and decorated with

red and green sugar crystals and silver balls, they carefully stacked them in tins. Callie always tried to hide the cookies.

"If we don't, the boys will eat them all in a few minutes," she said.

"Is that the Christmas spirit?" Grandma asked.

After the cookies were finished, Callie and Grandma went up into the attic to get the boxes of tree decorations. They sat at the kitchen table, carefully unwrapping precious ornaments one by one. Many of the handblown glass balls of yellow and blue and green were almost as old as Grandma. She and her sister Nellie had painted the fragile works of art when they were little girls studying at a convent school in a small town outside Rome.

Each ornament reminded Grandma or Callie of a story.

Grandma got tears in her eyes when she unwrapped the gaudy Styrofoam snowman Clint had covered with red and green glitter when he was in the first grade. Callie laughed at the sight of the lopsided snowman.

Her favorite ornament was a needlepoint angel with red yarn hair, blue eyes, and a long blue dress outlined with red holly and green leaves.

"Your mother made the angel the first Christmas after she married your father," Grandma told Callie. "She said she wanted a little girl who looked just like her."

Callie remembered one Christmas, when she was five or six, Santa left her a doll that was dressed just like the angel.

"I thought Santa was the smartest and most wonderful man in the whole world to bring me a doll with an identical dress," Callie told her grandmother.

Grandma just smiled. Callie knew now that it was Grandma who had made the dress.

Grandma always took a nap after they finished with all the preparations. Callie waited by the window for the rest of the family to return home. Darkness came so early on Christmas Eve, and it seemed forever until she heard Grandpa's pickup truck coming over the hill. Then she ran to wake Grandma.

The house was alive with excitement as everyone prepared for the evening ahead. First, they sat together at the table to eat Grandma's homemade chicken noodle soup and bread. Then Dad and Johnny went outside to the garage to bring in the trees. Grandpa always brought home the short-needled Fraser firs no one bought. The trees were scrawny, and some had big holes in the middle where branches were missing.

"We don't care how bare the tree is as long as it has a good, sturdy trunk," Dad would say.

Dad and Johnny sawed the branches off the different trees. Meanwhile, Grandpa used an electric drill to make holes about an inch in diameter and an inch deep in the trunk of another tree. Then Johnny and Dad would lay the cut branches into the holes. Slowly they created a tree that was picture-perfect. The finished decorated tree was always a miracle.

Grandpa always lifted the youngest grandchild above his head so he or she could put the needlepoint angel at the very top.

"This is the most beautiful tree we've ever had," Grandpa declared every year. And everybody would look at each other and smile and nod their heads in agreement.

This year Callie planned to carry on Grandma's tradition. She would bake the cookies and get the ornaments from the attic by herself. Grandma would want it that way. Callie couldn't think of changing it, not even by making a different kind of cookie.

"What kind of cookies are we going to bake if we don't have butter cookies?" she asked her mother as they put the last of the plates in the dishwasher.

"Mildred Dorsey told me yesterday her family loves a jelly-filled roll."

"Jelly!" Callie screeched. "Mom, nobody in this family likes jelly, not even for peanut butter sandwiches. Well, nobody except Clint, and we know how weird he is."

"Callie, that's not true. Grandpa spreads strawberry jam on his toast every morning. If you absolutely hate the idea of jelly cookies, I'm sure we can find something else."

Mom wasn't finished.

"When you're working on the lot this weekend, I want you to look for a nice, full white pine tree and put it aside. Your father can pick it up on Monday. We'll surprise Grandpa."

"White pine!" Callie screeched again. "Mom, Grandpa *hates* white pine."

"Now, honey, Grandpa doesn't hate any kind of tree. We always have the fir because it's the only kind of tree left on the lot on Christmas Eve. I personally don't like the fir tree because the tiny needles are so hard to clean up."

Callie poured detergent into the cup in the dishwasher door, slammed the door shut, and locked it. She pushed the buttons to turn it on, then spoke loudly over the grinding noise of the dishwasher.

"You're making a mistake, Mom. Grandpa hates white pine trees. He's told me a hundred times the only reason he has them on the lot in the first place is because they're good money makers. He says the Fraser fir is the only real Christmas tree in the world."

"Okay, okay," her mother said, throwing her hands up in exasperation. "Just pick out a pretty, full tree. I don't want to have to drill holes in the trunk on Christmas Eve and make a big mess."

Callie was waiting for just the right moment to ask her mother about going to Bethany's house. But now Callie couldn't even think straight. Her Christmas was crumbling apart. She didn't care what she said or when.

"With all the changes around here, I guess I won't have to work on the lots the weekend before Christmas," she said.

"Callie, what are you talking about? Of course you have to work. That's the biggest time of the year for us. We depend on every member of this family. Johnny's even coming home from Columbus to help."

"You're changing everything else. I didn't think it would make any difference to change that tradition, too."

"Camilla, what's gotten into you?" Mom asked. She looked hurt and angry. "We're changing some of our traditions to make it a bit easier on your grandfather," she explained. "He's having a hard enough time without being reminded every minute during the Christmas season of something your grandmother did with us. I would think you would understand that. As for the Christmas trees, the money we make sends Johnny to college and you to Dexter. I'm surprised at your quick tongue, and I'm disappointed."

"I don't care. I don't understand this at all. It just

isn't fair to change all the best traditions. Grandpa's going to hate it and be even more sad because we're forgetting every good thing we did with Grandma. We're forgetting Grandma."

Callie ran out of the kitchen and up the steps to her bedroom.

"Hey, shrimp, what's the matter with you?" Clint greeted her at the top of the stairs.

"Nothing. Just be prepared for the worst Christmas ever," she cried, slamming her door behind her.

chapter 4

Callie didn't sleep well that night. She was awake before Mom called her.

She pulled her green work sweater over her jeans and walked to the closet to get her boots. They looked just like the ones in her nightmare, except they weren't caked with mud.

Last night she'd had another nightmare.

She was outside Bethany's house, frantically pounding on the dining room window. But no one heard her because she had on Grandpa's brown cloth gloves.

Her friends were sitting at the long oak table. Their plates were filled with spaghetti and meatballs.

Everyone was trying to roll the spaghetti, but they didn't know how. Peter lost his grip on the big spoon and it flew into the air, landing on Bethany's plate.

Bethany looked shocked. Then she scowled and shook her finger at Peter. Callie couldn't hear what she said, but from the look on Peter's face, it must have been awful.

Bethany looked silly. A strand of spaghetti was stuck in her hair. Her white lace blouse was dotted with red sauce.

Callie knew how to roll spaghetti. "I can help you, I can help you," she mouthed through the window.

No one saw her except Ambrose. He just smiled his silly grin and rubbed his stomach to let her know she was missing a real treat.

That's when she woke up.

"Callie, Clint," her mother called. Callie ran down the steps.

The best part about selling Christmas trees was being with Grandpa. He had a way of making everything they did an adventure.

The family had three different lots in the city. Uncle Tony and Johnny worked the lot that was adjacent to a supermarket. Dad and Clint worked at another supermarket lot on the other side of the city. Callie and Grandpa worked at what used to be a gasoline station only a couple of blocks away from her school.

The first thing Callie and her grandfather did when they arrived at the lot in the morning was walk up and down the rows to make sure vandals had not stolen or damaged any of the trees during the night.

They had hired a security guard to stay in the

trailer and watch out for problems, but Grandpa never trusted the man to stay awake. This year he wanted to stay himself, but Dad and Uncle Tony had insisted he sleep at home.

"Waste of money to pay a security guard," Grandpa argued. In the end he listened to his son and brother. Clint promised that when he was sixteen he would stay and watch one of the lots.

"How about putting half of the holly wreaths on the table while I pull the pine roping up against the trailer," Grandpa said. "Remind me to tell your mother this afternoon that we need more roping from the other lots."

They didn't have to wait long for customers.

"How much are your holly wreaths?" asked a woman who was round and jolly like Santa's wife.

"Eight dollars. They come from North Carolina. Each summer my grandfather goes to a farm outside Raleigh to make sure we get the best trees and wreaths in town."

"That sells me. I'll take two. One for my front door and one for the back."

Callie took the lady's twenty-dollar bill and figured her change from the money in the cash box. This was the first year Grandpa had allowed her to work with the money.

"You've always been good with numbers," he told her. "If you want to be a doctor someday, you've got to be responsible. Don't tell your mother and father. This will be our little secret."

"That's seventeen, eighteen, nineteen, twenty dollars." Callie counted the money into the lady's hand. "Thank you. Can I help you to the car?"

"That's fine, I can carry them. Merry Christmas."

The lady passed Grandpa on her way out. "Great little salesgirl you have there," she said.

"The best." Grandpa beamed.

The church bells were ringing twelve before there was time for a break.

"Come on, Grandpa, let's eat."

Mom packed a lunch for them. Along with a sandwich and potato chips, she always included a surprise. Sometimes it was an apple or a pear or a bag of nuts. Callie hoped today's surprise was a brownie. A chocolate brownie would really lift my spirits, she thought.

Grandpa took off his brown cloth gloves and laid them on the table. He unsnapped his bib overalls.

"Do you want baloney and cheese or salami and cheese?" Callie asked, lifting a piece of the bread on the sandwiches her mother had neatly wrapped in aluminum foil.

"Salami for me. How about a cup of tea from the thermos? Do we have sugar?"

"Mom doesn't forget anything, Grandpa. She made hot chocolate, too. Would you rather have that?"

Grandpa shook his head.

Callie and Grandpa ate their sandwiches in silence. Callie glanced over at her grandfather. He was chewing his sandwich, staring into space, lost in his own world.

"I hate lobster," she blurted out.

"What did you say? Hate lobster? I didn't know you had ever tasted it."

"Well, I have, or I mean, I almost did once," she stumbled.

"Lobster meat is real good eating. I used to have lobster in my fish market. When your dad and his brothers were still at home, your grandmother and I had lobster bakes. I dug a pit in our backyard where we made a fire to boil the water for the lobsters. The meat is sweet and tender. Maybe we can have a bake sometime next summer."

"Don't do it for me. I won't touch the stuff. And you know Clint won't eat it. He's such a finicky eater."

"I'll insist you two at least try it. You can't say you don't like something until you've tasted it. Cracking the claws and digging the meat out takes some work, but it's well worth the effort."

"Is it hard to do?" Callie asked.

"At first. But I'll show you how."

The idea of Grandpa showing her how to eat lobster lightened Callie's mood. *I better come up with a real good excuse for not going to Ann's dinner* party, she thought. I don't want her to get mad and not invite me to her house next year when I'll know how to eat lobster.

Grandpa started to get up from the table.

"Hey, don't you want to see what our surprise dessert is?" Callie protested. She put the plastic-covered plate in the middle of the table.

"Let's see," he said, rolling his eyes and rubbing his chin. "Tapioca."

"Tapioca? Oh, Grandpa, get serious."

"Since this is Christmastime, how about your grandmother's famous butter cookies?"

"I seriously doubt it, Grandpa. Hurry, guess again."

"Brownies." He smiled like a kid who has just found a toy in his cereal box.

"Let's hope you're right."

Like a magician pulling a rabbit from a hat Callie lifted the top off the plate with a flourish. She looked, blinked, and looked again. There in the middle of the plate sat two limp, doughy rolls, oozing jelly.

"*Mmmm*, these are a surprise. What are they?" Grandpa asked, lifting one from the plate.

"Yuck. I'm not touching them. Mom's friend Mildred told her about the jelly rolls she always makes for Christmas. She probably gave Mom these to sample. Do they taste as awful as they look?"

"Not bad. Not good. They sort of taste like

something is missing from the recipe."

"You can have them both. I'm not hungry," Callie said, putting the napkins and paper plates into a bag.

Grandpa finished his tea.

"I hope your mother plans to make butter cookies," he said as they went back outside. "I was just thinking the other day how good they are."

"I don't know if she can make them this year, Grandpa."

"Well, if she doesn't have time, then you can make them. Grandma told me that someday you would probably make them better than she could."

"I don't know if I'll have time." Callie looked away.

"What's that? Doesn't this new school give you any vacation for the holidays?"

"It's just that there are so many other things to do. I'm already invited to two parties."

"Well, I hope somebody in this family has time to bake them. It won't be Christmas without 'em."

"Tell me about it, Grandpa," Callie said. But he didn't hear. He was already showing a tree to a customer.

chapter 5

Callie followed Grandpa across the lot. The clouds had cleared and the sun was shining. The sign on the bank across the street said it was ten degrees warmer than when they'd started work early in the morning.

Callie unzipped her parka and stuffed her gloves deep into her pockets.

All the talk about the butter cookies gave her an idea. She could take Grandma's cookie cutters to school for her Christmas tradition speech. I can make some dough the night before and show them how to roll it, she thought. I can borrow Mom's cutting board. I'll be like a chef on television!

The idea for the speech made her happy. But the thought of the jelly rolls put Callie in a bad mood again. I might as well pick out the tree Mom wants me to put aside to take home, she thought.

She walked up and down the rows. Mom didn't

like firs because she was still sweeping up needles in July. But Grandpa thought a tall, stately fir was the best for showing off their beautiful ornaments.

"Christmas trees should be decorated," Grandpa always said. "When the trees are too full, the ornaments get lost in the branches. It looks like you brought in a tree from outside and just strung some lights on it."

Of course, Grandpa never mentioned his personal preference when he was selling trees.

Callie looked at the different kinds of trees. The Scotch pine was beautiful and bushy with long willowy needles. Aunt Alice bought a pine every year. By the end of the holiday season more glittery balls were on the floor than on the tree. Clint always liked her tree best because it looked so silly with strings of lights and garland drooping off the limbs.

Callie tried to find a tree with needles that weren't too short or too long.

Then a picture of the disgusting jelly rolls flashed through her mind. Everything else is different this year, so the tree might as well be really different, too, she thought.

She picked the fattest, shortest tree on the lot. Now she had to find a place to hide it so no one would buy it before Dad took it home.

Callie was good at hiding things. Last summer she'd found the perfect denim wallet at Aker's

Department Store. She was ninety percent sure she wanted to buy it, but she had to check out what the other stores had before she counted out $7.95 of her hard-earned babysitting money.

She had slipped the wallet under the gaudiest yellow-and-pink flowered purse she had ever seen in her whole life. Aunt Martha gave Mom purses like it all the time and Mom never even took them out of their boxes. Callie knew no kid would ever look at something like that. Sure enough, when she returned thirty minutes later, the purse hadn't been touched and her wallet was still tucked safely beneath it.

She took a sales tag from her pocket, carefully printed $75 on it, and wired it to a tree limb.

On her way back to the trailer, Callie decided to move one of the fir trees to fill the spot that had been empty since Grandpa sold a balsam fir early that morning. The tree was twice as tall as she was. She grabbed onto the trunk and rocked it back and forth to move it along the asphalt pavement. It seemed to take forever.

Callie bent aside one of the branches to see if Grandpa needed any help with customers. Her heart stopped beating.

Not fifty feet away, Bethany and her father were walking toward her.

Callie froze. "I've got to get out of here!" she gasped.

She put her head down and slowly turned the tree around until her back was facing the Clarks. She inched the tree along the pavement until she found a clearing, then leaned the tree between two other trees. Keeping her back to the Clarks, she ran to the end of the aisle and dropped to the ground. She crawled to the trailer as fast as her knees would carry her and slammed the door shut.

Callie pressed her back against the door. Maybe if she didn't breathe and closed her eyes real tight she would disappear. It didn't work.

She turned and peeked out the window. The Clarks were talking with Grandpa. There were three other customers on the lot. Another couple was getting out of their car.

"Please make them go away," she prayed.

She peeked out the window again. Grandpa was walking toward the trailer. The Clarks were looking at a Scotch pine.

"Callie, Callie, are you in here?" Grandpa opened the door wide.

Callie kept her back to the door.

"I'll be right there, Grandpa."

"Hurry, we have lots of customers out here."

He left the door open. Callie backed up to the door and shut it.

I've got to do something quick, she thought. She zipped up her parka as she glanced around, taking in everything at the speed of a camera click. Her dad's old drab-green army jacket was draped across a chair. She put it on.

Jason's orange-and-black ski mask was lying under the chair. It was a tight fit, but she managed to stretch it over her face.

She grabbed her pink knit hat and pushed her hair up inside of it, then pulled up the hood on her parka and snapped it closed.

"Callie!" Grandpa yelled from outside.

She looked in the mirror. Perfect. Not even Mom would recognize her.

She looked down at her hands. Her emerald ring. Bethany would recognize it. In fact, Bethany, Ann, and Monica had all complimented her on the ring on the first day of school. She had explained it was her birthstone, but she didn't tell the whole story about the ring. Maybe she would have the chance to share that with Bethany when she stayed at her home overnight.

Quickly, she twisted it off her finger and pushed it into her pocket.

Callie tripped as she moved and almost fell out the door. I feel like an astronaut walking on the moon, she thought.

She kept her head down as she lumbered past the Clarks and Grandpa to a young couple who were admiring a tree that was twice their height.

"May I help you?"

They didn't stop talking or look at her.

"May I help you?" she shouted through the ski mask.

"Yes. We would like this tree right here," the man said. "Do you have some rope so I can tie it onto the top of our car?"

"Yes, I do."

She reached for the sales tag wired on a middle branch and yanked it. Both the tag and limb came off into her hand.

"Oh, no!" Callie cried. But the man and woman both laughed.

"That's okay," the man said. "This is our first Christmas tree and we really don't have enough ornaments to decorate anything this big."

"The tree reminds me of the ones my mother used to put up," his wife added. "It's nice and full. One less branch won't make a difference."

"The tree is thirty dollars, but I'll sell it to you for twenty-five," Callie said. Normally, she would get Grandpa's okay to lower the price. But he was still busy talking to the Clarks.

The man handed Callie a fifty-dollar bill before he took the tree to the car. Callie and the woman walked to the table. When Callie opened the cash box and took out the bills, she realized she only had tens and twenties, plus three one-dollar bills.

Oh, no, no fives, she thought. She closed her eyes tight. Now what should I do? She couldn't lower the price any more.

Then Callie remembered Grandpa had a roll of bills in his pocket.

"Are you okay?" the lady asked.

Callie opened her eyes.

"I have to ask my grandfather for some change."

"Your eyes look glassy. And why do you have all those clothes on? It's unseasonably warm today."

Callie didn't say a word. Instead, she walked sideways up to Grandpa, keeping her back to the Clarks.

"The short needles don't hide the ornaments," she overheard him tell Dr. Clark.

She tugged at Grandpa's overalls just like Jason did when he wanted his attention.

Grandpa turned to see who was pulling at him.

"Grandpa, do you have any ones?" she whispered.

"What did you say? Speak up, girl. What's the matter with you?"

"Do you have any ones or fives?" Callie said in a deep voice.

Grandpa dug deep into his pocket and brought out a thick roll of bills. "Why do you have on that heavy army jacket and knit hat? Aren't you hot?"

She didn't answer. He handed her three fives and

ten one-dollar bills. A five-dollar bill fell to the ground. The wind caught it and blew it in the direction of Dr. Clark.

Now what do I do? Callie wondered.

She pretended she didn't see the bill drop. Instead she walked as fast as she could back to her customer.

"Hey, wait. You dropped a bill," Dr. Clark called to her.

"Give it to my grandpa," she said without turning her head.

She gave the woman her change, grabbed some twine, and walked over to the car where the man was waiting.

"Aren't you hot in that hood and coat?" he asked.

"I'm just getting over pneumonia and the doctor said I should keep my head covered whenever I'm outside," Callie lied. She could feel the blood rushing to her face. She already felt weak from the heat.

"You shouldn't be working outside at all if you've been sick. I'm surprised your parents would let you do this work. It really is a boy's job."

"I can do it just as well as my brother Clint, even better," she snapped. "My grandfather says I'm the best salesperson he's ever worked with."

The man looked over at Grandpa, shook his head, and got into the car.

The Clarks were walking to their car empty-handed when Callie turned around. Grandpa was busy with another customer.

Callie watched the Clarks' car turn the corner and disappear down the street before she pulled the ski mask off and unzipped her parka. Her hair was plastered against her head with perspiration.

"Here, young lady, I would like this wreath," a tall, thin woman called to her.

Callie took her money and was standing by the cash box when Grandpa walked up.

"I swear I don't understand people," he grumbled, shaking his head. "I show people the best trees I have and they still aren't good enough. Or I should say people aren't willing to pay a reasonable price for the best tree."

Callie was thinking about Bethany's father. She had never seen him before. He hadn't come to the school's open house because he was at the hospital with a patient. Callie thought his pencil-line mustache made him look like a movie star.

"What did they say to you?"

"This last man was willing to buy the tree, but his wife said she saw a tree just as pretty on the lot downtown and it was half the price."

"What about the man with the girl? What did he say?"

"That cheapskate said the tree was exactly what he wanted until he saw the price. Then he said the tree was too skinny. He said he had an artificial tree at home that was twice as full. With the looks of that fancy car he's driving, he could buy our five most expensive trees with just the cash he carries in his wallet for an emergency."

"You didn't say anything like that to him, did you?"

She held her breath.

Grandpa hesitated a minute. He got a familiar sheepish grin on his face.

"I wouldn't do anything like that. I might have suggested he'd have a merrier Christmas if he had some Christmas spirit and a live tree."

Callie cringed.

She looked long and hard at Grandpa as he counted the money in the box. His bulky winter clothes underneath the gray overalls made him look twenty pounds heavier. He wore his billed cap pulled down to his eyes, and he had on brown work gloves.

Bethany would never recognize him if he was dressed normally, Callie decided. But in case he left a lasting impression, she thought it might be best not to introduce Grandpa to her for awhile.

chapter 6

Callie was so busy helping customers for the next three hours that she didn't have time to think about how miserable she was.

"Look at that, Grandpa," she said, pointing to a car that had stopped on the street to wait for a parking space. Three cars were backed up behind it. The driver in the second car was blowing his horn. "We're causing a traffic jam!"

Grandpa smiled. "Callie, could you wait on those people over there? I want to take the money I have in my pockets and some of the money we have in the cash box and put it in our hiding place in the trailer."

Callie walked over to a lady with snow-white hair dressed in a hunter-green coat with fur at the collar and sleeves. She was standing by a white pine. "May I help you?" Callie asked.

"Yes, I like this tree," she said. "What do you think, Billy?" She looked at a boy who had blond hair and blue eyes just like the man who stood next to him.

"I like it, Grandma. Do you think there's enough room under the limbs for Santa to put my gifts?"

"I'm sure there is, dear. Yes, I think it's perfect. We'll take it."

The lady followed Callie to the table while the man and boy went to get the car. "I do this every holiday season at the same time," the woman explained. "In my family it's a tradition that I take my youngest grandchild with me to pick out my tree. Then we go home and decorate it. Actually, I need the children's help with the tree, but I never tell them that. They think it's because Santa comes to my house early."

The lady smiled and winked at Callie. Callie tried to wink back, but she didn't have her heart in it.

Just the mention of a family Christmas tradition made Callie sad again. As she watched the grandmother and her family leave the lot, she wondered if she would be able to keep any of her family's traditions this year. Mom had made it clear that there would be no butter cookies and that she wanted a different kind of tree. What else would she change?

❊ ❊ ❊

"This was one of the best Saturdays I can remember in a long time," Grandpa told Dad when he came in the van to pick them up at the end of the day.

Callie smiled. Grandpa said that every year.

"Hi, Callie," Mom greeted her as she climbed into the van. "Did you have a busy day? You look tired."

"We sure did. Grandpa said it was the busiest day he can remember in a long time."

Mom gave her a knowing look and they both smiled.

This was Callie's favorite time of the day. They stopped selling trees a little before dark. Mom drove to each lot and picked everyone up. By the time she got to the lot where Callie and Grandpa were, every seat was taken and they had to squeeze in.

They all acted like they hadn't seen each other in weeks. They spent twenty minutes telling stories about their day on the lot. Sometimes everyone talked at once, and they all laughed a lot. Dad would start singing, "Jingle bells, jingle bells, jingle all the way," and they'd all join in.

Callie didn't see Johnny until she was inside the van.

"Hi, Camilla," he said, giving her a big hug and kiss. She loved how her name sounded when he pronounced it.

"Johnny, you're home," she said, throwing her arms around his neck. She snuggled in the seat beside him. Johnny had a partial scholarship to the state university and Callie really missed having him at home.

"Glad to see you made it, son," Grandpa said, shaking Johnny's hand as he took the seat behind him. "Did you have trouble getting a ride home?"

"He didn't even start until five this morning," Mom said. "Ask him what he did last night."

Everyone turned to Johnny and waited for his answer.

"One of the girls in my introductory physics class asked me to her sorority's Christmas party."

"Johnny's got a girlfriend, Johnny's got a girlfriend," Clint chanted.

"Shhhh, Clint. Don't be so obnoxious," Callie scolded.

Johnny was very shy and hadn't dated much in high school. Callie remembered the time her parents asked him to take the neighbor's daughter to her prom. He was so nervous he cut himself shaving and had red blotches all over his face.

Mom and Dad didn't seem upset that Johnny stayed in Columbus to go to a Christmas party, Callie thought. Of course, he wasn't expected on the lot on Friday and he was home in plenty of time to work today.

Maybe she could talk Mom into letting her go to Bethany's about four o'clock on Saturday. That way she'd only miss a couple of hours of work on the lot.

And she could tell Bethany that Mom had to pick her up early Sunday morning because her family was going to be with her grandfather, something they did every year on the Sunday before Christmas. That certainly was the truth. She didn't have to say *where* she spent her time with Grandpa.

The fact that she had to be with her grandfather on Sunday was the excuse she would give Ann, too. For all Ann knew, Grandpa might live in Columbus, which was a two-hour drive each way. She couldn't expect Callie's family to come back early because of the party. And no one could get upset with her because she was going to visit her grandfather.

She leaned back in her seat, feeling smug.

"I was afraid Callie was going to have heatstroke," Grandpa's booming voice broke into her thoughts. "The bank sign across the street said it was fifty degrees and there she was all bundled up in her parka like it was below zero."

"Were you chilled?" Mom asked.

"I think I'm getting a little bit of a cold." Callie blushed with the lie.

"We'll take your temperature when we get home. This is good pneumonia weather."

"I'm okay. Really, Mom."

"What she needs is some of Grandma's good chicken noodle soup," Grandpa said. "Grandma always said that would fix anything that ailed you."

Everyone grew quiet at the mention of Grandma's name. Grandma had a talent for understanding and taking care of them all in her special way. She always had hot chocolate and freshly baked chocolate chip cookies waiting for them when they got home from working on the lots.

Mom seemed to sense what everyone was thinking.

"I have a roast in the Crock-Pot, and I'll make some soup. For dessert I have some more of Mildred's delicious jelly rolls."

"Oh, yuck," Clint said under his breath. Only Callie and Grandpa heard him. Grandpa smiled.

Callie looked at Clint in surprise. Maybe he's got some taste after all, she thought, and found herself grinning.

chapter 7

Johnny helped Dad carry wood into the house to start a fire in the fireplace. Mom went to the kitchen. Grandpa and Callie started up the steps to change their clothes.

"Oh, Callie, you got a telephone call from Bethany Clark today," Mom called from the kitchen.

Callie stopped dead in her tracks. Grandpa bumped into her and almost lost his balance.

"Sorry, Grandpa. What did she want, Mom?"

"She wants you to call her. She said something about ice skating next week."

Callie walked down the steps and into the kitchen where Mom was standing at the stove stirring the soup.

"Did Bethany ask where I was?" Callie asked as casually as she could. She opened the refrigerator door and pretended to look for something to eat, but all the while her heart was pounding.

"Yes. I told her you were with your grandfather at the Christmas tree lot. She said she and her father were going to look for a tree today, too."

"Is that all she said?" Callie scooped some cottage cheese onto a dish.

"Camilla, you're going to spoil your dinner. Now go upstairs and change your clothes. I need you to pour the milk."

"I'm starved, Mom. A few bites of cottage cheese won't spoil my dinner. Did Bethany want anything else?"

"No, that's all. Now hurry, Callie, and make sure Grandpa doesn't take a nap. He needs a good, hot dinner."

Everyone was hungry. They ate in silence.

"We've all had a long day," Dad said. "You all hurry on upstairs and get into bed. I'll help Mom with the dishes."

"Thanks, Dad," Callie said, leaning over to kiss her father good night.

Callie didn't even bother to take off her jeans or sweater. She was asleep the minute her head hit the pillow.

❋ ❋ ❋

"Camilla. Camilla. It's time to get up," Johnny said, knocking gently on the door and opening it at the same time. "It's seven o'clock. Can you hear me?"

Callie rolled over. She opened one eye to look at the clock on the nightstand. Where did the night go? She felt like she'd gone to bed just a few minutes ago. At least nightmares hadn't interrupted her sleep.

"Come on. I want to see both eyes before I leave."

She opened both eyes wide and gave her favorite brother a big smile.

"I'm awake," she said as he started out the door. "Johnny, how did you get Mom and Dad to agree to let you stay in Columbus long enough to go to that party?"

"I just told them the truth. I have classes until five-thirty on Fridays and Mom knew I'd arranged a ride home with my roommate, Scott, early in the morning. Why do you ask?"

"Oh, I was just wondering."

"I know better than that. I'll bet you're up to something." Johnny turned to walk out of the room, and Callie hopped out of bed. Maybe tonight would be a good time to ask her parents' permission to go to Bethany's house.

It was drizzling rain when Mom dropped them off at the lot in the morning. By midafternoon the rain had turned to sleet. No one was buying Christmas trees, so Dad and Grandpa closed the lots early and headed home.

Callie went to her room to finish her homework. When she was done, she went downstairs to help Mom peel the potatoes.

"Did you find a tree?" her mother asked.

"Yes. It's a white pine. I hid it behind some trees in the far corner of the lot and put a seventy-five-dollar price tag on it. Dad can't miss it."

"Good. I'll tell him where it is and he can bring it home in the van tomorrow. I want to get started making those jelly rolls. I can bake them tomorrow and freeze them. Everybody seems to like them."

"You mean you're going to bake before Christmas Eve?" Callie was shocked.

"Honey, you know there's always so much work at the last minute. Mildred bakes right after Thanksgiving, so I'm getting a slow start. I want us to have a very calm Christmas this year."

"Sounds boring to me."

"Now, Camilla, we've gone through this before. Let's not start again."

"I think Grandpa will have a fit when he finds out what you're planning. I know he's going to hate the tree. And yesterday he said the jelly rolls tasted like something was missing."

"Really? Your dad said they were good. I know it's hard, Callie, but we have to change our routine as much as possible. We have to think of Grandpa."

"What are you thinking about me?" Grandpa

asked, walking into the kitchen.

"Grandpa, you can't ask a question like that at Christmastime," Callie teased him.

"Okay. Then can I ask when dinner is? I'm *huuuuungry.*" Grandpa drew out the word like Jason would, making Callie giggle.

"It'll be about fifteen minutes," Mom told him.

Grandpa walked over to the stove, lifted the lid on the pot of steaming tomato soup, and stirred it.

"*Mmmm,* looks good. I think I'll have a bowl right now. Don't worry, it won't hurt my appetite." He smiled, answering the unasked question.

"Say, Dad, what did you think of the jelly rolls?" Mom asked as she took dishes from the shelf.

"They were okay."

"Just okay? Mildred sent them over to us. Her family loves them."

"Maybe her family doesn't know what's good like we do. Those rolls certainly don't compare to your brownies or Grandma's butter cookies."

Callie smiled. Mom frowned. Grandpa slurped his soup.

I'm glad we came home early from the lots today, Callie thought. When I ask to go to Bethany's everybody will be in a good mood, not sleepy and ready to fall into bed.

She pictured them in her mind: Dad, Grandpa, and Uncle Tony leaning back in their chairs; Mom sipping a second cup of coffee; Clint and Johnny drooling over a second helping of apple cobbler.

I don't know how I can lose, Callie thought. The first time Mom or Dad says no, I'll remind them that Johnny got to stay in Columbus to go to a Christmas party. The second time, I'll say Clint is on the school track team and one of them has to drive him back and forth after school and on weekends.

And if all that fails, I'll bargain with them, Callie decided. I'll baby-sit Jason any time they want for all of January and February. That'll get them.

The dinner started at a leisurely pace. But they weren't even to second helpings when things started to go wrong.

The doorbell rang. Scott had come early to pick up Johnny. The roads were slick, and he wanted to take his time driving back to school.

Johnny was barely out the front door before Clint piped up.

"Hey, Dad. You promised to play a game of chess with me when you had some extra time, remember? How about right now?"

"Are you sure you're ready for this?" Dad teased.

"You bet."

"I'll play the winner," Uncle Tony said.

"Hey, what about dessert?" Callie asked.

It was important that everyone be at the table when she asked the question. She knew there would be a discussion and that everyone would have to agree that letting her go to Bethany's house was the only fair thing to do.

They all looked at Mom.

"Just for tonight you can take it into the TV room," Mom said.

Dad and Clint filled their bowls with big helpings of cobbler and started to leave the kitchen.

"Call me when you have a winner," Uncle Tony said.

"Me go, too, Daddy," Jason said, jumping off his chair.

"Mom, do we have to take him? He'll ruin everything. He always wants to play and knocks the pieces off the board," Clint complained.

"No, that's okay. He has to finish his dinner," Mom said. She had to promise Jason that she would watch cartoons with him before he stopped crying.

"When are you and Callie going to make those butter cookies?" Grandpa asked, leaning back in his chair.

"I was going to make some jelly rolls tomorrow. They can be frozen. But you told me you didn't like them."

"We can have both. Why don't you let Callie make the butter cookies? Her grandmother told me last year it wouldn't be long before she wouldn't be needed in the kitchen at all. Callie could bake them alone."

"I don't know if Callie will have the time. She's busy at school and the tree lots and I need her to help with the house."

Callie started to say she would find time. But she closed her mouth. I better watch out, she thought. Mom will say I can't go to Bethany's because I have to bake cookies.

The mention of jelly rolls reminded Grandpa of a story about homemade gooseberry preserves his family used to buy from a man who lived in a mountain shack outside Charleston.

Callie listened impatiently to Grandpa's long story. Uncle Tony remembered the man and added more to the story that Grandpa had forgotten to mention. She kept wondering when they would finish.

Jason had eaten all the potatoes on his plate and was crying because he wanted to watch cartoons. Mom had one eye on him and one eye on Grandpa. She looked like she wondered when he would finish, too.

Callie knew the minute Grandpa stopped talking Mom would be up, taking Jason into the family room. She had to ask the question now.

"Your grandma always liked the—" Grandpa was saying.

"Mom, I've got to ask you something," Callie burst in, almost shouting.

"Camilla. You interrupted your grandfather."

"That's okay. I'm finished."

"I was wondering, since we're changing things around this Christmas, would it be okay if I got off early the Saturday before Christmas and spent the night at Bethany Clark's house?"

"Changes? What changes are we making?" Grandpa asked.

Callie knew that would get Grandpa's attention.

"Camilla, although you didn't mention you were invited to Bethany's house, I thought I had answered that question a couple of days ago," her mother said. "That Saturday is the busiest day of the year. Why can't you understand that?"

"Because it isn't fair. Bethany Clark is the most popular girl in the class. Her parents always let her ask one friend to stay overnight the Saturday before Christmas. If I don't go, she won't invite me to another thing. And nobody else will either because she'll tell them I'm not allowed to do anything."

Tears started to well in Callie's eyes, and her voice cracked.

"You let Johnny stay in Columbus and you let Clint be on the track team. All I ever do around here is work. And all you want to do is change our family traditions. I think you're mean. You don't think about anybody but yourself."

Callie pushed her chair from the table and started to leave the room.

"You sit right back down young lady," Grandpa commanded. "I will not have you talking to your mother like that. You apologize to her."

Grandpa never got angry. Callie sat down and buried her face in her hands.

"I'm sorry, Grandpa, but—"

"Don't tell me you're sorry. Tell your mother."

"I'm sorry, Mom. But I didn't get invited to the Halloween party and everybody else went. They're always talking about going to each other's house and all the fun they have."

Callie hesitated.

"I don't really think you're selfish," she finally said.

No one said a word for several minutes. Even Jason sat quietly. Dad and Clint stood in the doorway. They must have heard Grandpa raise his voice.

Mom got up and started clearing the table.

"What do you say, Kathleen?" Grandpa asked. "Callie makes a good point. She has worked hard, and she's been a big help to me. This is the first thing she's asked to do."

"Dad, you know how busy we are that Saturday."

"That's true. But Clint can ask one of his friends to help and Johnny can bring his roommate home from college."

No one said a word for what seemed like forever.

Grandpa broke the silence. "Kathleen, let me tell you a little story."

Oh, no, Callie thought. Not another one of Grandpa's long stories!

"My baby brother Tony here was a good athlete when he was a kid. Could have been one of the best football players in Dodge County. The coach wanted him to go to a football camp in the summer to learn some of the finer points of the game and to get into a muscle-building program. The coach came to our fruit market and asked our father to give him a week off from work. Our father said he could develop all the muscles he ever needed by lifting the crates in the store. Tony never went to camp or played football."

"John, I didn't know you remembered that," Uncle Tony said, obviously touched by what Grandpa was saying.

"I never let on. I respected Dad and loved him. But this was one time when he was wrong, Tony."

An awkward silence filled the room. Callie forgot about going to Bethany's house and looked at Uncle Tony. "I'm sorry that happened to you," she said.

"I didn't know you were an athlete," Clint said, walking into the kitchen and sitting down next to Uncle Tony. "And the best in the county."

"Oh, that was a long time ago," Uncle Tony said, embarrassed by all the attention.

"Maybe you could help me with my running and we can toss balls. What do you say?"

Uncle Tony put his arm around Clint and smiled at Grandpa.

"Are you sure you can handle it if the boys help?"

Grandpa nodded.

"Joe, is it okay with you?"

Dad nodded.

"Well, okay. But Camilla, I must say that I am very upset by your outburst."

"Oh, thank you, Mom. Thank you," Callie said, kissing her mother on the cheek. Then she threw her arms around Grandpa's neck, almost knocking him off his chair. "Thank you."

She kissed Uncle Tony on the forehead.

Callie ran out of the room and up the steps two at a time. She grabbed the phone and quickly punched in Bethany's number.

"Hello, Bethany. This is Camilla. My mom said you called. Guess what? I can come to your house for sure. Early afternoon will be perfect. Did you have any doubts?"

chapter 8

The freezing rain turned to snow. By morning, the countryside looked like a soft white blanket.

In the city, the snow had transformed the bare trees and drab, cold asphalt into a winter wonderland.

Callie looked over at Mr. Gordon's evergreen tree as she walked into school. The colored lights looked like giant gumdrops against the snow. You were right, Mr. Gordon, it is beautiful, she thought to herself.

Callie could feel the upcoming holiday excitement when she entered her homeroom class. Everyone seemed to be talking and laughing at the same time.

Mrs. Peterson rapped the palm of her hand on her desk. "Class, may I have your attention. Please, take your seats. I know it's hard to concentrate so close to vacation time, but we have a lot of work to do."

The room quieted.

"Our special Christmas program in our chapel is set for December twenty-third. As you know, we depend on you and your families to donate the wreaths, trees, holly, garland, all the things that we need to decorate the chapel. Many of you have been very generous, but we still need a few more decorations to make it as beautiful as it can be."

Peter Hall raised his hand.

"My father said he'll give the poinsettias again this year."

Peter's father owned the largest florist business in the city.

"Thank you, Peter. We were counting on that."

Callie loved the school's chapel, which was used as an assembly room for special occasions. The room was long and narrow. Sunlight poured through the stained glass windows, casting red, green, and yellow shadows on the old oak pews and shining hardwood floors. The chapel had been built in the late 1880s and was one of the few rooms in the school that hadn't been destroyed by a fire in the 1930s.

Callie could picture the chapel dressed in holiday greenery. She raised her hand.

"Yes, Camilla," Mrs. Peterson said.

"My family would like to give the Christmas trees."

When Mrs. Peterson first mentioned the need for trees, Callie hadn't volunteered. That was weeks ago when she was seriously considering telling her parents that she didn't want to return to Dexter the next semester. But things were going so much better now, she couldn't imagine any reason why she wouldn't return in January.

"Camilla, that's wonderful and most generous. But trees are very expensive. Can somebody else also bring trees? We need fifteen. The faculty usually chips in to buy one or two."

"Oh, that's not necessary. I'm sure my family can come up with enough."

Bethany, Ann, and Monica all turned around in their seats and smiled at Callie.

"My grandfather has this thing about Christmas trees. He just loves to buy them."

Callie didn't add, "He also loves to sell them." She didn't even blush.

"As long as you don't believe it will be too much for your family, we'll put you down for fifteen trees. We've never had all the trees we needed. The chapel will be its prettiest ever, thanks to Camilla and her family. Class, let's give Camilla a round of applause for her generosity."

Callie could feel her face turn red. She kept her eyes on her desk, too embarrassed to look up. No one had ever clapped for her before.

"Class, we won't have our family tradition speeches today. Instead, we'll go to the chapel and practice our vignettes. This will be our first rehearsal in front of the whole class."

"That was really nice of you to give the trees," Bethany said as she waited for Callie to get her books from under her desk. "I know how expensive trees are. My dad and I looked at trees this weekend. He thought the prices were outrageous and he wouldn't buy one. Mom and I were disappointed because we wanted a live tree this year, but Dad said no."

"Really? Grandpa thinks the trees are priced just right this year." Callie smiled.

Monica was waiting for Callie at the chapel door. "Do you think everybody knows what they have to do, Camilla?"

"I'm sure they do," Callie said with a confidence she didn't feel.

Most of the class was already seated. Ann waved Bethany over to the seat she had saved for her. Monica squeezed in next to Peter. Callie was still standing alone in the back when Mrs. Peterson called Bethany and Ann to the front. Callie took their place in the pew.

"Mrs. Peterson," Bethany said when she got to the podium. "Ann and I had an idea for something we can do for everybody as part of our Hanukkah presentation. One of the customs during this eight-day celebration is to play a game with a dreidl."

Ann held up a four-sided top. "Each side has a letter. In Yiddish they mean 'nothing,' 'everything,' 'half,' and 'put one in,'" she explained. "All the players put an equal number of something—for example, chocolate pieces—into a pot and keep a certain number for themselves."

Bethany held up a coin the size of a fifty-cent piece. "This is really chocolate covered with gold foil." She removed the paper and popped the morsel into her mouth. "*Mmm*, good," she said. Everybody laughed.

"The players take turns spinning the dreidl and must do whatever it says on the side that comes up," Ann continued. "The player with the most chocolate at the end wins."

"What we would like to do after our presentation is share the chocolate coins with the audience," Bethany said. "We'll fill a basket with coins. Then we'll ask the youngest member of each family to stand up and catch one. What do you think?"

"Yes, yes," the class approved.

"Girls, that would be a lovely little gift for our families, and a great way to end the sixth grade's program," Mrs. Peterson said. "We'll switch the presentations so you will follow Monica and Camilla."

Mrs. Peterson noted the change on a piece of paper.

"Okay, Camilla and Monica, is your group ready to perform your vignette?"

I'm glad we won't be following Ann and Bethany, Callie thought as she walked to the front of the room with Monica, Melissa, and Patty. Ambrose followed, carrying a stepladder.

Callie and Monica walked to the podium and faced the class. Ambrose set up the ladder in the middle of the stage, then walked behind the curtain with Patty and Melissa.

"This is the story of mistletoe," Monica began.

"Louder, Monica. Remember how we practiced? I want to hear everything you say from back here," Mrs. Peterson called out.

"This is the story of mistletoe," Monica repeated in a stronger voice.

On cue, Patty, draped in a pink sheet covered with white beads, walked onto the stage. On her head she wore a wire wreath with an antenna that moved back and forth when she walked. At the tip of the antenna she had attached a sprig of mistletoe.

She climbed to the top of the ladder.

"Mistletoe is a parasite that grows on apple or oak trees. It got its name from the mistle thrush, a bird that feasts on mistletoe."

When Monica said "thrush," Patty pulled out a stuffed bird from under the sheet and held it high. The bird hit the antenna and flipped the wreath to the floor. Patty looked down, horrified. Everyone started laughing.

"Mistletoe has always been associated with peace," Callie continued, her voice shaking. Mrs. Peterson had coached them if anything went wrong, they couldn't stop. "Remember the show must go on," she had said.

"Calm down, Camilla," Mrs. Peterson warned.

Callie took a deep breath and continued. "In olden days when there were great battles, warriors would stop fighting when they got under a tree that had mistletoe in it. They would call a truce."

Callie paused. Nothing happened on stage.

She looked at Monica. Monica looked at her. "They would call a *truce*," Callie shouted.

Still nothing happened. She was just about to repeat the line when Melissa and Ambrose came out from behind the curtain. Each was wearing a suit of armor cut out of cardboard and a football helmet covered with aluminum foil.

They clanged their long toy swords together as they moved across the stage. When they got next to the tree, they suddenly stopped dueling, dropped their swords, and put their arms around each other.

"Let's not fight anymore," Melissa said for everyone to hear.

She smiled at Ambrose. But he wasn't looking at her. Instead he was looking out at the audience.

He was white as a ghost, and his brown eyes looked like saucers. He didn't move.

"Ambrose, I said let's not fight anymore," Melissa shouted.

Ambrose was in a stupor. With a sinking feeling, Callie realized he had stage fright.

"Ambrose, you're supposed to say 'Let's be friends.' Remember? How can you be so stupid?"

The word *stupid* got Ambrose's attention.

"What did you call me?" he said.

"Stupid."

"I am not," he shouted. "You're the one who's stupid. In fact, you are so stupid that I don't want to be up here with you. Find another friend."

As Ambrose hurried off the stage, he stepped on Patty's wreath, squashing the mistletoe berries under his shoe.

Patty screamed, "Ambrose, you're not only stupid, you're clumsy, too!"

Melissa started to cry.

Callie shook her head in disbelief. This was as bad as her nightmare. Only this was real life. The whole class was laughing at everyone on the stage.

"Students, please," Mrs. Peterson said, walking down the aisle from the back of the room. "It seems we need a little more practice with our mistletoe presentation."

As Mrs. Peterson talked, Patty started to climb

down the ladder. When her foot hit the floor, she tripped on the sheet and fell into Melissa, who was caught off balance. Melissa and Patty fell into Monica and Callie and knocked over the podium. Everybody went crashing to the floor with a thud.

"Hey, you guys are funny. This is better than television," Michael Farrell shouted.

"Class, please," Mrs. Peterson said. "These things will happen. Please find Ambrose, and the five of you meet me after school so we can practice some more."

"I don't want to be in a program with that jerk Ambrose," Melissa said. "Can't we get somebody who can remember a few simple lines?"

"Now, Melissa."

"Melissa's right, Mrs. Peterson," Monica said. "Ambrose is a real nerd. It was Callie's idea to ask him to be in our play."

Callie didn't like the way this conversation was going. "But you agreed to ask Ambrose," she protested.

"Girls, please. We will talk about this later." Mrs. Peterson turned to the class. "Peter Hall and Dennis Clark, are you ready for your presentation?"

* * *

Later in the morning, Callie caught up with

Ann Layman at the salad bar in the cafeteria. "Ann, thanks a lot for the invitation to your house," she said. "I'd like to come, but that Sunday my family is going to visit my grandfather in Columbus. I tried to change the day, but you know how it is around the holidays. You do the same thing every year at the same time. My grandfather is a bit cranky and would be very upset with us if we didn't come like we always do."

Once Callie started talking, she couldn't stop. By the time she was finished her face looked like a red beet, but Ann didn't notice.

"I'm sorry. Maybe next time." Ann picked up her tray and walked to a table where Monica and Bethany were sitting. She didn't ask Callie to join them.

That didn't surprise Callie. She knew Monica blamed her for the disaster during the rehearsal.

It doesn't matter, Callie told herself as she sat at a table with a girl from her math class. I'm going to Bethany's house, and that's more important.

During the drive home from school, Callie told her mother about the rehearsal.

"Ambrose made a fool of everybody, Mom. It was awful. And then Monica got mad at me. Ambrose said he was sorry, and Mrs. Peterson told us we have to keep him in the play. It's going to be a disaster."

"I'm sure everything will be just fine," Mom said.

"I'm not. Ambrose is a nerd. He reminds me of Clint. Maybe you shouldn't come to the program. You might be embarrassed."

"You would never embarrass us, Callie. In fact, the whole family is planning to go. And we're all looking forward to it."

chapter 9

Callie was busy the rest of the week in school. Time passed quickly.

After dinner on Friday, Callie went up to her room to pack and lay out her clothes for the next day.

She had talked her mother into letting her wear her new purple corduroy slacks. They were perfect with the pink sweater her grandmother had knitted for her last Christmas.

Callie took her new cherry-red flannel night-gown, an early Christmas gift, out of its plastic bag and put it at the bottom of her suitcase. She put the plastic bag in the top drawer of her dresser to save it. She'd promised Mom she would wrap the gift and put it under the tree.

"I promise I'll act surprised," she told her mother. "Going to Bethany's house is my Christmas gift."

She neatly folded her underwear and socks and tucked them along the sides of her suitcase. As she snapped it shut, she noticed her emerald ring wasn't on her finger.

She looked in her jewelry box. It wasn't there. She hurried to the bathroom. Maybe she'd taken it off when she washed her hair. She pulled back the shower curtain. There was no ring on the ledge.

Callie ran down the steps to the kitchen. Maybe she'd put the ring on the windowsill when she helped Mom peel potatoes.

The spindly, half-dead cactus Clint had won at the school festival last year was the only thing sitting on the sill.

Callie got a funny feeling in the pit of her stomach.

Grandpa had given Callie the ring the day they had buried Grandma. It was wrapped in tissue paper inside a tiny silver case that Grandpa had given Grandma for their fiftieth wedding anniversary.

The emerald set in antique gold had been Grandma's engagement ring. Grandpa chose emerald because it was Grandma's birthstone, and they had gotten married on her birthday.

Grandma had let Callie try it on only once.

"Someday it will be yours," Grandma promised. "But don't tell anyone. It will be our secret."

Somehow Grandpa knew about their secret.

"You and your grandmother shared lots of things, including birthstones, and I know she wanted you to have this," Grandpa had told Callie when he'd given her the ring.

"I'll keep it forever and never take it off," Callie had said.

"Never is a long time," Grandpa had said and smiled.

Now, not even six months later, Callie didn't know where the ring was. If only she could think *why* she had taken it off, maybe then she could remember *where*.

She didn't hear her mother walk into the room. "I thought you would be asleep by now," Mom said to her.

"I needed a glass of milk," Callie lied. She couldn't tell Mom she was looking for the ring.

"I'll take everyone into the city tomorrow and then go to the supermarket," her mother said. "I should be home about eleven, and we'll go to Bethany's about noon."

"That sounds great. Good night, Mom."

Callie hurried up the stairs, almost spilling her milk. She rushed over to her dresser and looked on the little gold jewelry tray where she kept her honor pins from school. No ring.

She couldn't think of anyplace else to look.

* * *

The next morning, Callie awoke with the nagging fear that she might never find the ring.

She pushed back her blanket, grabbed her robe, and walked over to the window. It had snowed most of the night.

"Are you up, Callie?" her mother asked, knocking on the door and opening it at the same time.

"I'm almost dressed."

"Did you hear the phone ring late last night? It was Johnny. They had so much snow in Columbus yesterday that the state highway patrol closed sections of the interstate."

Callie stopped buttoning her blouse. "Does that mean he isn't coming home?"

She held her breath.

"He said he and Scott will leave just as soon as they can. But they'll be late. Your dad, grandfather, and Uncle Tony said they can handle the lots until Johnny gets here. Clint's friends have promised to help, too."

Callie was thinking about the ring when she met Grandpa at the top of the stairs.

"Penny for your thoughts on this beautiful snowy morning?" he asked her.

She couldn't tell Grandpa about the ring. "Oh," she stammered. "I was just thinking how much I like snow and how much I love you." She flung her arms around his neck and kissed him on the cheek.

"Thank you, Callie. I love you, too," Grandpa said, obviously pleased with Callie's sudden burst of emotion.

At the breakfast table, Dad, Grandpa, and Uncle Tony made a bet on how many trees they would sell. Dad predicted at least seventy-five.

"I say twice that many," Grandpa said.

"Joe, you don't have enough, and John, you're too high," Uncle Tony said. "I say ninety-five to a hundred."

The talk about trees reminded Callie of decorating the chapel for the Christmas program. "I almost forgot to tell you," she interrupted. "They decorate the chapel at school for our Christmas program. I told Mrs. Peterson our family would—"

Before she could finish, the phone rang. Clint jumped up to answer it, knocking his glass of milk into Callie's lap.

"*Cliiinnntttt,*" she screeched, jumping up to get a towel.

By the time she remembered to ask about giving the trees to the school, everyone was already in the van. I'll tell Mom when she gets home, she thought.

Jason didn't want to go outside and play in the snow. He just laid on the couch with his blanket, watching cartoons.

"Are you sick, little guy?" Callie said, feeling his

93

forehead with her hand like Mom did. "You do feel a little warm." She sat on the couch with him until he fell asleep.

A little while later, the telephone rang.

"Camilla, this is Johnny. Is Mom or Dad there?"

"No. They've already left for the lots. Are you almost home?"

"This zero-degree weather zapped Scott's car battery. We couldn't jump it with cables, so now we're waiting for someone from the service station to get here. We hope to get out of here by noon and home by four. I hope it doesn't put everyone in a real bind. I know this is our busiest day."

"Dad and Grandpa said they can handle it."

Callie was dressed and ready to go when her mother walked into the kitchen with a grocery bag in each arm.

"Mom, Johnny called. He said Scott's car has a problem with the battery. He'll be a little late."

"The side roads are snow-covered, but the inter-state traffic is moving well. They won't have any problems if they can get the car started," Mom reassured her.

"I think Jason is sick. He didn't want to go outside."

Mom went to check on Jason. Callie brought the rest of the bags into the kitchen and put the groceries away.

"Thanks, Callie," Mom said, walking into the kitchen. "I think Jason just has a cold. I'll bundle him up when we go out. It's almost twelve. We'd better get started."

Callie went upstairs to get her suitcase and skates. As she started back down, the phone rang. She hurried into her parents' bedroom to answer it, thinking it might be Bethany.

But as Callie put the receiver to her ear she heard her father saying, "Kathleen, we've got problems. Clint seems to have a bug. He's thrown up twice and his forehead is warm. He needs to be in bed. Only one of his friends from the track team showed up to work and Uncle Tony needs him on his lot. Dad said we've got people walking off the lot because he can't wait on them."

Callie put the receiver down and walked slowly back to her room. She took off her corduroy slacks and sweater and threw them on the bed. She grabbed her jeans out of the laundry basket.

She was rummaging through the bottom dresser drawer for a heavy wool sweater when Mom walked into her room.

"I heard, Mom. I'll call Bethany and tell her I can't come."

"I'm sorry, Camilla. I really am."

Mom tried to put her arms around Callie, but Callie brushed past her. She was afraid she would start to cry if she let her mother hug her. She went into her parents' bedroom and closed the door.

"Bethany, this is Camilla. I've got some bad news. I can't come over to your house today. My cousins from Maine . . ."

She paused just long enough to calm herself. Her heart was racing. Her palms were sweaty. Lying wasn't going to get her through this situation.

She took a deep breath and started again. "My grandfather needs me to help him work on our Christmas tree lot in the city."

"What Christmas tree lot? What are you talking about?" Bethany asked.

"Oh, I thought I told you. My grandfather, well, actually my whole family, sells Christmas trees. It's great—"

"Can't you go tomorrow?"

"No, I have to be there today *and* tomorrow. This is the biggest weekend of the season. I usually—"

"Can't you get somebody else to work for you?" Bethany's voice was rising. "Ask your brother."

"I can't. He's sick. That's why I have to go."

"I just can't believe you are doing this to me, Camilla," Bethany snapped. "It's too late to ask anyone else. My mother and father made all these plans just for you and me. You've ruined my weekend."

"I'm sorry," Callie said. But Bethany didn't hear her. She'd already hung up the telephone.

chapter 10

Callie sat in the van, quiet as a mouse. Tears rolled down her cheeks.

"I know how you feel, Callie," her mother said.

"No, you don't. Not only will I never be invited to Bethany's house again, she'll never talk to me and neither will anybody else. You should have heard her on the telephone. She was so nasty. She hates me. I don't want to go back to Dexter next semester."

"Now, Callie, you're upset. Let's think about this."

"No, Mom. Our family is not like her family. Bethany's family makes plans to do something and then they do it. We never know what we're doing. Something's always messing up our plans at the last minute."

Her mother had no answer.

Clint was bundled in a blanket when he came out of the trailer to the van, and he looked pale. "I feel awful, Mom," he moaned. "I threw up my toast and eggs in the trailer and Grandpa had to clean it up."

"Oh, gross, Clint. You're making me sick," Callie complained. She was too miserable to feel sorry for him.

Grandpa was busy with a customer and waved when Mom pulled the van up to the lot. Callie jumped out, slamming the door behind her. She didn't say good-bye.

She waved at Grandpa and walked toward a lady who was admiring a white pine. The tree was short and round. So was the lady.

"My husband took one look at the snow this morning and said forget the artificial tree," the lady told her. "He's even buying new ornaments."

Callie helped the lady carry the tree to her car. The tree was short enough to fit in the trunk. Callie tied the hood down with twine.

She met Grandpa on the way back to the lot.

"What brings you here? Weren't you planning on going to your friend's house today?"

"Everything has gone wrong today, Grandpa. Johnny is still in Columbus and when Dad called to tell us Clint was sick, I knew I had to come help you. You can't do it alone on the busiest day of the year. It really doesn't matter anyway. Bethany will never talk to me again."

"I doubt if it's that bad."

"You don't understand! You're just like Mom," Callie exploded. "Other people make plans and stick to them, but not us. Bethany's family buys their plane tickets for Utah in October. Our family doesn't even know what we're doing on Christmas Eve."

"Well, now, you're wrong there. We always know what we're doing on Christmas Eve. We bake cookies and put up our scraggly tree and make it look beautiful. I took the electric drill over to the repair shop last week, just to make sure it doesn't conk out on us at the last minute."

"You don't have to worry about your old drill."

"What are you talking about?"

"Oh, Grandpa, haven't you noticed? Mom and Dad are changing everything this year."

"What do you mean? Changing what? Why, for heaven's sake?"

"Because, because—"

As if a dam had broken, she couldn't hold back the tears. They poured down her cheeks in streams. Grandpa put his arms around her while she sobbed.

"Now, now, Callie, tell me what the matter is. What did I say? What's going on in this family?"

Callie buried her head in his shoulder.

"Excuse me," a man called.

"I'll be right there," Grandpa shouted. "Honey, there's a man who wants a tree. Take this and dry those tears. I'll be right back."

Callie took Grandpa's handkerchief and wiped her face. The bitter cold made the tears sting on her skin. She blew her nose before she stuffed the big white handkerchief into her jeans pocket.

The truth hit Callie like a bolt of lightning. She had shoved her ring into her pocket the day she was trying to hide from Bethany.

Callie tore off her gloves and felt in all her pockets. The ring wasn't there.

Callie ran to the trailer. Dad's army jacket was lying on the chair. She went through the pockets, but the only things she found were a hard piece of gum, a tag, and some wire.

She got down on her hands and knees and crawled around the floor. She looked under the couch and down between the cushions in the stuffed chair. Nothing.

Callie went outside and tried to remember where she was standing while she was hiding from Bethany. But it was useless. The ground was now covered with snow and ice. If the ring had fallen out of her pocket, she wouldn't have a chance of finding it until next spring.

"Young lady, could you please help me?" asked an elderly woman who was looking at a tiny fir.

Callie was busy for the next hour with a steady stream of customers. She didn't have time to talk to Grandpa.

Light snow started falling late in the afternoon. Callie tried to help a man and his wife, but she could tell from the way they talked that they would never agree on one tree. Grandpa had taught her that when customers started to argue it was best to leave them alone.

As she walked to the trailer, Callie kept her eyes on the ground. The green emerald could show up against the white snow.

She walked right into a customer.

"I'm sorry." She looked up at a tall man who reminded her of Peter Hall. Standing next to him *was* Peter.

"Hey, is that you, Camilla? Hi."

"Hello, Peter," she mumbled.

"What are you doing here? Looking for a tree?"

"Well, umm, sort of. My grandfather and I are, ummmm . . ."

"They really have a lot of trees here. The best my dad and I have found anyplace in the city."

"You think so?"

"I know so. Well, I've got to go, Dad's ready to leave. Nice seeing you, Camilla."

"Bye, Peter."

By early evening there were another two inches

of snow on the ground. Mom surprised Callie and Grandpa by picking them up early.

Callie dragged herself to the van. She was tired and sore from lugging trees and hoisting them into car trunks. She rested her head on Grandpa's shoulder and fell sound asleep. She didn't even remember her father picking her up and carrying her to bed.

❀ ❀ ❀

When Callie woke up the next morning she was burrowed under two quilts. Her clock read 7:30.

"Oh, no! I overslept!" Callie cried. She threw off the covers, grabbed her robe, and ran to the window. A new thick blanket of snow stretched as far as she could see.

Callie hurried out into the hallway. There wasn't a sound. The doors to Mom and Dad's room and Clint's room were closed. Johnny's door was open, and his bed was still made. He hadn't made it home last night after all.

Callie tiptoed down the steps. She could hear Dad, Grandpa, and Uncle Tony talking in the kitchen. They were sitting at the table, drinking coffee, when she walked into the room.

"Wow, did you look outside? Isn't this great?"

"We're snowed in," her father said.

"No, we aren't, Joe, You know my truck. It can get through anything once I get a good start."

Grandpa's beat-up, dirty white truck was about thirty years old. The inside was worn and rust had eaten away some of the floor around Grandpa's seat. Callie loved to sit up front next to Grandpa and watch the pavement pass beneath the truck as they drove along. The muffler made a horrible roar. Everyone could hear Grandpa coming before they saw him, but he bragged that, although the truck looked bad, it was more reliable than Dad's new car. One day last year the family had to ride to the city's July Fourth celebration in the pickup because Dad's car wouldn't start.

"I heard the snow plows out on the main roads about four this morning," Uncle Tony said.

"What's the point of trying to fight this? We should just stay home today. I'm sure we won't have enough business to make it worth going into the city."

"What's the point?" Grandpa echoed. "We'll sell out of trees today, Joe. People love to go out in inclement weather. Makes 'em feel like pioneers. They get the Christmas spirit. An artificial tree is good enough in fifty-degree weather. But when the earth is covered with snow on the outside, nothing but a fresh tree will do on the inside."

Uncle Tony nodded, agreeing with Grandpa.

"John, remember that year the city had a snow emergency, but people bought trees and took them home on their sleds?"

"I'll never forget it. We sold every tree that year."

"Grandpa and Uncle Tony are right, Dad," Callie said. She poured herself a glass of orange juice and sat down at the table with them. "We were so busy yesterday I never sat down once. I didn't even get to eat my sandwich until after four o'clock."

Realizing he had two allies, Grandpa kept talking.

"Even if we don't open the lots, I have to go into the city to meet a florist. He ordered twenty trees to decorate the ballroom at a downtown hotel. He's coming by this afternoon with his truck."

The only florist Callie knew was Peter's father. "Is that the man who was on the lot yesterday with his son?" she asked.

"Yes. The boy said he knew you from school."

"Did he say anything else?"

"When he said he knew you, I told him you're my granddaughter and the best salesgirl I've had in my fifty years selling trees."

"He told me that we had the best trees in the city."

"No doubt about that."

Callie drank her orange juice and thought about

Peter. Dad, Grandpa, and Uncle Tony sipped their coffee and stared out the window.

"Hey, where's Mom?" Callie asked.

"She's sick today," her dad said. "She must have caught that bug from Clint. I want to give her a chance to get some rest. She's worn out."

"Dad, why don't you stay here and let me go with Grandpa and Uncle Tony?" Callie asked. "I really don't mind."

"Sounds like a good idea to me, Callie," Grandpa said. "What do you say, Joe? Tony will handle the lot on Monmouth Street. Callie and I will go to our lot. We won't stay if there isn't any business."

Callie knew Dad wouldn't say no. She hurried upstairs to dress.

❋ ❋ ❋

Grandpa's truck made it through the snow, although it took twice as long to reach the city. The truck got stuck in a snowdrift once and Callie and Uncle Tony had to get out and push.

"Okay, push on the count of three," Uncle Tony said.

Callie had never seen Uncle Tony so animated.

"You love this, don't you?"

"Callie, your grandfather and I have been getting in and out of trouble together for over half a century."

The city streets were almost deserted, but people were waiting when they drove up to the lot. Callie spent the morning waiting on customers. Every time she moved a tree or picked up a garland from the ground, she looked to see if the ring was underneath.

The clock was striking two o'clock when Peter drove up with his father in a big flatbed truck. Callie didn't recognize him at first. Peter was wearing overalls, and dark green rubber boots almost reached his knees. The hood of his parka was pulled over his head, and he had on brown cloth gloves just like Grandpa's.

"Hi, Camilla," he greeted her.

"Hi, Peter."

"How's the tree business?"

"Well, I don't really know. I just help Grandpa when it's absolutely necessary."

Callie hesitated. She was tired of lying.

"Actually, I've been selling Christmas trees since I was a kid. Grandpa talked my dad into selling trees as a family business. Every year Grandpa drives to North Carolina to order them. We have acres and acres of pines planted on our property so we can sell our own trees someday."

"That sounds like a lot of fun. Do you go to North Carolina with your grandfather?"

"He's promised to take me next year."

"Peter, come help me," his father called. Grandpa was up on the truck and Peter's father was handing trees up to him.

"I've got to go now. Maybe sometime I could talk to you and your grandfather about the tree business. I want to have my own florist business someday. Maybe I can grow trees, too."

"I helped plant the little seedlings. I can teach you about that part."

"That would be great,"

Callie watched Peter jump on the truck where he stood next to Grandpa.

Bethany, Ann, and Monica talked about Peter a lot at school, but Callie hadn't spoken to him much before today. He was very friendly. She liked the way he used his hands when he talked. She liked his smile, too. She wondered if she smiled at him enough when he talked to her.

The rest of the day was uneventful. By dusk the temperature was near zero and they were nearly sold out of trees.

"Look at this scraggly tree," Grandpa said, holding up a skinny fir that had only a few branches. "This will be perfect for filling in our tree."

Grandpa tossed the tree in the back of the truck. He shut the gate but it didn't catch. It never did.

Callie climbed into the passenger seat. She knew she should tell Grandpa about the short, fat white pine tree that Dad had put in their garage, and about the cookies and the ring. But she was too tired.

Then she remembered the school Christmas program.

"Oh Grandpa. I forgot to tell you. I promised my teacher that I would bring the trees to decorate the chapel."

"How many trees are we talking about?" Grandpa asked.

"They need fifteen."

"Callie, we don't have fifteen good-looking trees on all three lots. We're down to almost nothing."

"But Grandpa, we've just got to find the trees," Callie begged. "The whole class heard me tell Mrs. Peterson that my family would bring them."

"Can't you tell them we've run out and we'll give them as many good ones as we have?"

"No. I sort of made a real big deal out of it. I said you enjoy buying Christmas trees."

"Buying and selling. We don't normally give them away. If I felt that way, we wouldn't have a business. I just don't understand what you told your friends."

"They're not my friends."

"No? Peter is a fine young man."

"Peter is different. I wanted everyone to think our family is special. I thought if we donated the trees, they would like me."

Grandpa looked over at her as if he wanted to say something. Then he just shook his head and stared out the windshield. They rode in silence to the lot where Uncle Tony was waiting.

Callie moved closer to Grandpa on the seat to give Uncle Tony room. "I'll do what I can, Callie," Grandpa said. "But I can't make any promises."

chapter 11

No one had to wake Callie the next morning. She dressed quickly and hurried downstairs. Dad was sitting at the table eating a bowl of cereal.

"Is Mom still sick?" Callie asked as she popped two pieces of wheat bread into the toaster.

"She's feeling a lot better, but I wanted her to sleep in this morning. She's got a busy week ahead of her. I'll take you to school."

"Where's Grandpa and Uncle Tony? Aren't they up either?"

"Grandpa was up at the crack of dawn and is already gone. Said he had some things to do in the city. I haven't seen Uncle Tony this morning."

Callie and her father ate their breakfast in silence. And neither one said a word on the ride into the city. Callie was tired and disappointed. It wasn't anyone's fault but her own the way the weekend had turned out, she thought. I never should have begged to go to Dexter.

Callie kissed her father on the cheek as she got out of the car. He looked tired. "I love you, Daddy."

"Love you, too. Have fun today."

As luck would have it, Callie met Bethany on the steps. "Hi, Bethany," Callie said softly.

Either Bethany didn't hear or pretended she didn't. When she saw Callie, Bethany turned her head and hurried up the steps.

Callie acted like she didn't notice and lagged behind. She kept her head down so she wouldn't have to talk to anyone and walked straight to her locker. She slipped into her seat at the back of the room just as the final bell rang.

Bethany was sitting up front. Ann Layman was right next to her. They had their heads together, talking about something.

"I want to tell you how pleased I am with your sharing family Christmas traditions," Mrs. Peterson began. "We've had Christmas in our class for more than a month. We still have to hear from Sam Schmidt and Camilla Thomas."

When Mrs. Peterson mentioned her name, Bethany, Ann, and Monica turned around in their seats and glared at her. Peter also looked her way.

He was smiling.

"If Camilla and Sam don't mind, I would like to wait for their presentations. Instead, I think we need to go back to the chapel and practice our part in the school's Christmas program. I was disappointed in the way our first dress rehearsal went."

This time everyone looked at Ambrose. Callie did, too. He didn't seem a bit embarrassed.

"It wasn't my fault," he said.

"Was, too," Melissa said from the corner of the room.

Oh, no, they're at it again, Callie thought.

"Class." Mrs. Peterson rapped on her desk for attention. "We're not placing blame. We just have to make sure we do a good job on Wednesday night. We don't want our class to be the laughingstock of the school. Now hurry, I've already taken up too much time."

Callie was halfway down the hall when she heard Ann call her name. She looked around. Ann and Monica were walking toward her.

"I guess I know now why you didn't come to my party." Ann said. "Bethany told us how you couldn't come to her house because you had to help your grandfather sell Christmas trees. I thought you were going to Columbus to visit your grandfather. What happened?"

Callie couldn't think of a thing to say.

"Bethany is really upset," Monica added. "You should have heard what she said to us. Her mother and father were so angry. They couldn't understand how you could let them make plans when you knew all along you couldn't go."

"You were really rude," Ann said.

"I didn't know I couldn't go," Callie tried to explain. "It was at the last minute when everything went wrong."

But they weren't listening. "You really missed a good party at Ann's, too," Monica turned to tell Callie as she walked away. "Everybody was there."

Callie stood in the middle of the hallway while the rest of the class walked around her. She could feel the tears welling up in her eyes. She couldn't let anyone see her cry.

Instead of turning right to go to the chapel, Callie turned left and ducked into the restroom. But Mrs. Peterson saw her and stuck her head around the door. "Hurry, Camilla. We need everyone to practice."

Billie Simpson and Mary Morris were finishing their presentation when Callie trudged into the chapel. Peter was sitting near the door, reading his notes. "Hi Camilla. I was looking for you," he said.

Oh, no, he's mad at me for something, too, Callie thought. "Hi, Peter," she mumbled, trying to act uninterested in anything he might have to say.

"I wanted to tell you the trees looked great in the ballroom at the hotel. I know the manager liked them a lot. Tell your grandfather, will you?"

"Thanks. I will."

"Hey, are you okay? You don't look so good. Don't worry about Ambrose. I'm sure he'll be okay today. He just got nervous in front of everybody. He's funny that way. But he's really an okay guy."

"I hope you're right."

Before Callie could say anything else, Mrs. Peterson called Peter to the front of the chapel.

Callie slid into Peter's seat. She looked around the room. Monica was sitting up front with Bethany and Ann. She wondered how Monica would act when they were called to do their presentation.

"Camilla, can you move over a little bit?" It was Ambrose. Callie considered telling him to find another seat, but then moved over. Maybe if she was nice to him, he wouldn't get upset.

"Are you ready?"

"Yep. I don't think I'll be nervous today. And it was Melissa's fault. She thought everything I did was stupid."

"I doubt that," Callie said.

"She did. Trust me. I didn't tell anybody but she made fun of the helmets. She said they looked stupid. It was my idea to cover them in foil."

Callie could tell Ambrose was getting upset

again. "Well, I think the helmets were very, ummm, very creative." Callie chose her words carefully.

"Did you really think so?"

"Yes, I did."

Monica didn't wait for Callie or Ambrose when Mrs. Peterson called their names. She was already standing at the podium and didn't speak when Callie took her place next to her.

"This is the story of mistletoe," Monica began slowly.

The play moved along as they had practiced it and Callie began to relax.

"Let's not fight anymore," Melissa said to Ambrose, as they stood under the mistletoe.

"Right. Let's be friends."

The class, remembering the first rehearsal, cheered when Ambrose said his lines. Ambrose was embarrassed by the applause but he obviously liked it. He liked it so much that he forgot to follow Melissa offstage. He stood alone, grinning like a little boy with a big chocolate ice cream cone. Callie waited for Melissa to come back onstage and claim Ambrose before she started her next lines.

"Mistletoe still is a symbol of peace and love. We hang sprigs of mistletoe in doorways and on chandeliers. It's an accepted custom that if people see someone they like under the mistletoe, they can steal a kiss."

On cue, Melissa and Ambrose strolled hand in hand onto the stage. Patty, who was sitting on top of the ladder, pulled out a heart-shaped piece of red cardboard and held it in front of her face. With her other hand, she held out sprigs of mistletoe that were tied together with a red ribbon.

Melissa stopped under the mistletoe, closed her eyes, and puckered her lips.

Ambrose stopped dead, looking at Melissa with a dazed expression. Callie held her breath and closed her eyes. Kiss her, she wished. Kiss her, Ambrose.

"Yuck, they're really going to K-I-S-S," Marvin Foster shouted from his second-row seat.

Oh, no, here we go again, Callie thought.

Ambrose looked out into the audience. But this time he didn't panic. Instead, he smiled. Then he turned his head, leaned over, and planted a kiss right smack on Melissa's lips.

Callie forgot herself. "You did it, Ambrose. You did it!" She started to clap and so did everybody else. Some of the boys whistled.

"Much, much better," Mrs. Peterson said from the back of the room. "Now if we can do it just like that on Wednesday night for our families everything will be perfect."

Callie turned to Monica to give her a high five. But Monica was gone. She was already walking out the door with Bethany and Ann.

✽ ✽ ✽

Wednesday was the last day of school. Callie was getting books from her locker when the principal's voice rang out over the public address system, reminding everyone that classes would be dismissed at one o'clock.

Rats, Callie thought. I forgot to tell Dad that I get out early. Now I'll have to sit and listen to everyone else's big plans for the holidays. That is, if anyone is still talking to me.

She slammed her locker door shut and headed off to class.

"I want to tell you how pleased I was with the rehearsals," Mrs. Peterson said. "You all did a great job. Just remember to speak loudly and slowly tonight and don't get nervous. Now we're going to finish sharing our family traditions. Sam, will you begin please?"

Callie felt numb. She had forgotten about her speech. She grabbed her backpack and frantically started looking for her props.

She had put the cookie cutters in her pack last week. She pulled them out one by one. First a star, then a tree, a stocking, and a wreath. She put them on her desk. Now to find the Play-Doh that she'd decided to use instead of real dough.

It wasn't there. Jason must have taken it out to play with. It was his Play-Doh after all.

Callie looked around the room. Everyone was paying attention to Sam. The door was less than three feet from her desk.

I could leave and no one would know or care, Callie thought. When Mrs. Peterson comes looking for me I'll tell her everybody in our family is sick and I had to throw up.

"Thank you so much, Sam," Mrs Peterson said. "Now, last, but not least, we'll hear from Camilla."

Callie got up from her desk and walked to the front of the room. She could see Bethany whispering something to Ann.

Callie felt like she was walking in glue. Her heart was pounding beneath her blouse. She reached Mrs. Peterson's desk and slowly turned to face the class. She knew exactly what she was going to say.

"For as long as I can remember our family's Christmas tradition has been selling trees," she began. "My grandfather buys them in North Carolina every summer. Trucks bring them to our house the week before Thanksgiving. There are many different kinds of trees."

Callie pointed to the tree decorated with strings of green, red, and blue lights in the corner of the classroom. "That's a white pine. You can tell by its long needles."

Callie used the blackboard to draw the different kinds of tree branches and needles. She could hear her voice getting stronger and stronger. And with her back to the class, she wasn't as nervous.

"And that's our Christmas tradition," she finally said, putting the chalk down on the tray and turning to face the class again.

There at the back of the room stood Grandpa. He was wearing his bib overalls and rubber boots. His cap was pulled down to his glasses.

Callie had no idea how long he had been standing there. He was smiling.

"Class, this is Camilla's grandfather," Mrs. Peterson said. "He's brought the trees to decorate the chapel, and he needs some help bringing them in."

Peter was the first to stand up.

Grandpa recognized him. "How are you doing, son? Did the trees look good in that fancy hotel?"

Ambrose and four other boys stood up and walked out of the room with Peter. Grandpa walked up to the front of the class where Callie stood.

"Callie, let me tell you what I want to do," he began. Everyone looked surprised to hear her nickname.

"I was only able to come up with ten good trees.

But I brought along some scraggly ones and the electric drill. You and I can fill in the trunks so they look nice and full. When you're finished here I'll be waiting for you in the chapel."

"Gee, Mr. Thomas, can I help, too?" asked Peter, who had come back into the room. Grandpa nodded. Together they went into the hallway.

Callie started toward her seat.

"What an interesting talk," Mrs. Peterson said. "It seems we left the best and most traditional celebration for last. Your family certainly captures the spirit of Christmas. Thank you, *Callie.*"

When Callie reached her desk, she heard the sweetest sound of her life. Her classmates were clapping for her.

She was so surprised, she didn't say a word. She just stood at her desk for a minute, basking in their sign of approval. Then she picked up her backpack from the floor and started toward the door.

"Callie." Callie turned to look at Monica. "It's okay if I call you Callie, isn't it?"

"Oh, sure. My family and, ummm, friends do."

Before Monica could respond, Melissa hurried over to ask a question. "Callie, I want to know about the trees. I never knew there are so many different kinds."

"Where is your family's lot?" Donald Lurie

asked. Callie couldn't remember Donald ever talking to her before.

"We've got three lots at different places in the city," she said. "I work at the one off Eighth Street."

"I wish I'd known that," Ann Layman interrupted. "We could have bought our tree from your family. The one we have is so ugly. Next year we'll buy one from you for sure."

"Next year," Callie repeated.

Callie answered everyone's questions before she looked at her watch. She had to hurry. Grandpa was waiting.

Monica met her in the hallway outside the chapel. "Callie," she started again. "I thought your speech was the best one of all."

"Thanks, Monica."

"And, Callie . . ."

Callie held her breath, waiting for Monica to finish.

"I'm sorry I was so rude and blamed you when the rehearsal turned out so awful."

"Oh, that's okay. It was my fault anyway. I suggested we ask Ambrose to be in the vignette for the wrong reason. He's such a nerd I thought it would be funny when he had to kiss Melissa in front of everybody."

"I thought it would be funny, too."

"Yeah, but the joke was on us. It turned out

okay, though. Ambrose isn't as much of a nerd as we thought."

"Hey, are you calling me names?" It was Ambrose, who was trying to aim a fat tree through the door to the chapel.

"Never, Ambrose," Callie and Monica said in unison. They moved aside to give him more room.

"I've got to go, Callie, but I'll see you tonight," Monica said as she turned away.

Callie followed Ambrose into the chapel, where he leaned the tree against the wall with the others. Peter was looking for a place to plug in the drill. All the boys were gathered around Grandpa, who was explaining exactly how he would drill the holes in the tree trunk. Callie just stood and watched. Grandpa didn't need her help.

Grandpa drilled the first few holes, then let the boys take turns drilling more.

"What do you think?" Grandpa called when he noticed Callie. "We need this kind of help at home."

"Oh, Grandpa, the trees look wonderful. Thank you so much."

Callie and Grandpa were moving one of the trees when Bethany came up to them. Callie stiffened, but Bethany was smiling.

"Live trees are so beautiful. They smell so good," Bethany said, sniffing the needles. "Every year I beg my parents to get a real tree. But Dad always says that because we fly to Utah on Christmas morning, it's a waste of money and too much work. Just once I wish we would stay home and have a tree and Christmas like everyone else."

"Really?" Callie said. "Would they let you keep a live tree if someone gave you one?"

"I think so. Why?"

"Well, maybe . . ." She turned to ask Grandpa if she could give Bethany the tree in their garage. But Grandpa wasn't there. She looked around the room and spotted him near the door.

"Wait here a minute, Bethany," Callie said and hurried over to Grandpa.

"I'm getting ready to leave," he said. "I'll be back about one o'clock to pick you up."

Callie walked with Grandpa to his truck. "Where are you going now?" she asked.

"Your mom still feels a little weak. I told her I'd go to the grocery store for her."

"Grandpa, I better go with you. You don't go to the supermarket very often."

"I know, but I'm giving myself some time to find everything. The things I can't forget are flour and a lot of butter."

"A lot of butter? What for?"

"Butter is a very important ingredient in your butter cookies. Right?" Grandpa's eyes were twinkling.

"Yes, but . . ."

"Your mom wants to help you make the cookies."

"Really?" Callie couldn't believe it.

"She told me this morning what she and your father were trying to do, changing everything around so I wouldn't miss Grandma so much."

"What do you think of their idea?" Callie asked.

"Not much. I told her that you can't change traditions like you change your clothes. Traditions are a part of each of us. They're gifts we give to each other year after year. Grandma helped us make our family traditions over the years."

He reached into his pocket to get his keys.

"Oh, yes." He turned to Callie. "Close your eyes."

He took her hand and dropped something tiny into it. She knew what it was before she looked.

"Grandpa, my ring!" she exclaimed. "You found my ring. Where was it?"

"It was lying on the floor in the trailer. I found it almost a week ago. I was waiting for you to ask me about it."

"I was afraid to tell you I had lost it," Callie said. "The only reason I took it off in the first place was because I was afraid Bethany would recognize it that day she and her father came to our tree lot. I was trying to hide from her. I didn't want her to know my family sells Christmas trees. Wasn't that silly?"

Grandpa didn't say a word.

"I've been so mad at Mom and Dad for trying to change our traditions and forget Grandma. But when I took off the ring I was doing the same thing." Callie went on. "I tried to shove who I am into my pocket. And I promised you I'd never take that ring off. Oh, Grandpa, I'm so ashamed. And I was so mean to Mom. Will she forgive me?"

"Why don't you talk to her about it when you're rolling out the cookie dough?" Grandpa suggested. He put his arm around her shoulder and together they walked to his truck.

Suddenly Callie remembered Bethany.

"Grandpa, I was wondering. Do you think we could give the pine I picked out for our family to Bethany? Then we could make our own perfect tree like we always do."

"Can't," Grandpa said. "That tree is already standing in the living room pretty as a picture. I'll bet your mom and dad will have it decorated by the time we get home."

"But Grandpa, making our own tree was a tradition. Grandma's tradition."

"I know, I know. But your grandma asked me for years to bring home a beautiful tree that didn't have to be fixed at the last minute. It was always such a messy job and it took a lot of time. She always wished she could have the tree up and decorated before Christmas Eve so we all could sit back and enjoy the evening."

"She never told me that."

"She didn't dwell on it, but I knew. Every year I'd promise her I'd get a tree next year. I'm finally making good on that promise."

Callie thought hard for a moment. "Then do you think we could give Bethany a tree from the lot?" she asked. "She's never had a live tree and—"

"Callie, I brought the last of our trees to school. I'm sorry, honey."

"That's okay, Grandpa," Callie said, trying to hide her disappointment. "I didn't promise her anything. It's just that she's my friend, and I feel bad for her. Can you imagine not having a tree? It wouldn't be Christmas."

Grandpa got into the truck, closed the door, and started the motor. Callie stood back.

Suddenly, Grandpa rolled down his window. "I have an idea," he shouted over the noise of the muffler. "Some of the seedlings we planted years ago at the house are just the right size for your friend. Ask her to come home with us. We'll let her pick a tree and I'll chop it down for her. I don't think anybody would object, do you?"

"Grandpa, that would be wonderful," Callie said, leaning inside the window to give him a kiss and hug.

Callie stood and watched until the white pickup was out of sight. She could hear the giggles of some kids who had stopped to watch the old, rusty truck that made such a loud noise.

"My grandpa just borrowed—" she started, then stopped. "That's my grandpa," she said proudly, turning to hurry back into the building. She didn't want to miss decorating the chapel. And she had to tell Bethany about the tree. Grandpa would be back to pick them up in an hour!

Callie was ready to celebrate the holidays.